THE STORY OF CROMWELL

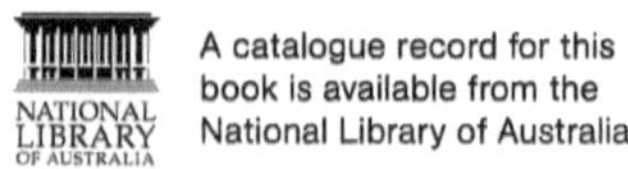

A catalogue record for this book is available from the National Library of Australia

THE STORY OF CROMWELL

HENRIETTA E. MARSHALL

PLEASE NOTE

In this series, you will read about historical figures who displayed courage, bravery, self-sacrifice, and many other admirable traits. Their stories remind us that many people in history took bold actions and made tough choices. Yet, even those who achieved great things sometimes held ideas or pursued goals that were not beneficial to everyone. History is full of complex individuals—parts of their lives inspire us to be brave and stand up for what is right, while other parts remind us to consider the unintended consequences of our actions.

As you explore these biographies, we invite you to reflect on the qualities that enabled these figures to achieve greatness and the lessons we can learn from their mistakes. Maybe you too can become a History Shaper—someone who learns from the past and helps to make our world a better place for everyone.

CONTENTS

CROMWELL AS MEMBER OF PARLIAMENT.

Chapter 1.
CHILDISH DAYS

ON the 25th of April 1599, more than three hundred years ago, when the great Queen Elizabeth was still on the throne of England, a baby was born in the little country town of Huntingdon. Four days later, the tiny baby was carried out of the goodly house at the end of the long straggling street, and taken to the Church of St. John to be christened. "Oliver" was the name given to the baby, and it was a name with which, forty years or more later, all England was to ring. For this tiny baby grew up to be Oliver Cromwell, Lord Protector of England.

Oliver's father was named Robert and his mother Elizabeth. Before she married her name had been Elizabeth Stewart, and some people say that she was a distant relative of James Stewart, King of Scotland, who afterwards became King of England too. But people only like to believe this because it is curious to think that, in days to come, Oliver Cromwell helped to bring his own distant cousin to death.

The house where Oliver was born is still pointed out in Huntingdon. But we can hardly tell what it looked like on that spring morning, so long ago, for it has twice been pulled down and built again. The church too in which he was christened has now disappeared. But some things are still unchanged. The town, with its one long, narrow street and irregular market-place, is much the same as when little Oliver was first carried out into the sunshine.

The Great Ouse still glides slowly by the town with many windings and twistings, from where it rises in Northampton, until it takes a sudden bend northward, and flows sluggishly onward, through flat fen-lands to the Wash.

The Fens, upon which little Oliver looked out from his nursery windows, were black marshes, here and there covered with stagnant water. There by day was heard the dreary cry of wild water-fowl, and there by night the treacherous will-o'-wisp gleamed and flitted. Now, Huntingdon is a farming county, for the fens have been drained, and where only water-fowl cried and will-o'-wisps danced, sheep and cattle graze, corn ripens, and comfortable red-roofed farm-houses dot the flat lands.

We know but little of what Oliver did when he was a boy. But he must have had some good times, for his grandfather, Sir Henry Cromwell, lived at the great house of Hinching-brooke, only a mile or two away. There little Oliver would pass many a happy hour.

There is a story told—I will not say that it is a true one—of how, one day, when Oliver was still a baby, he had been taken to see his grandfather. He lay asleep in his cradle, and his nurse must have been careless, for he was left all alone. As he lay there, a monkey came lolloping into the room and right up to the cradle. The monkey thought that the baby would be a lovely plaything, so he seized him and ran away with him. Leaping, swinging, clinging with hand and tail, he swung himself and his prize up to the flat lead roof of the house.

Soon the baby was missed, and when it was discovered that the monkey was playing with him on the roof, the whole household was thrown into a state of confusion. Beds and blankets were brought out and placed on the ground, to catch the baby, in case the monkey should drop or throw him down. But the monkey was careful, and presently he brought Oliver safely to the ground again. So the baby was saved to grow up to be a great man.

Sir Henry Cromwell lived in very fine style and spent a great deal of money. He was so grand indeed that he was called The Golden Knight. When Oliver was nearly four years old his grandfather "The Golden" died. We can imagine the stir in the great house, the comings and goings, the grave talks, sad faces, and little Oliver among it all hardly understanding what it meant. But perhaps he would cry a little, when he was dressed in black, and told that he would never see his kind grandfather again. He still went often to Hinchingbrooke however, for his godfather, Uncle Oliver, now lived there. And Uncle Oliver was almost as splendid and fine, and as kind to little Oliver as his grandfather had been.

Then one day there was again much stir and bustle in the great house. The best silver was brought out, the best silken robes and draperies. Every one was busy, hurrying hither and thither, full of anxious preparations. For why? The King was coming.

The great Queen Elizabeth was dead, and the new King, James, was journeying from Scotland, to claim his crown. Everywhere, in each town and village as he passed, he was greeted with shouts and cheering. The people hung out flags and made their houses and streets gay, and the lords welcomed him to their castles. Everywhere there was hunting, balls, and parties, but nowhere was there greater splendour than at Hinchingbrooke.

Just two days after Oliver's birthday, the King came. We can imagine how the little four-year-old boy would watch, as the gay procession came along the road. The glittering dresses, prancing horses, flashing armour, the noise and dust, the clatter and jangle would be something to think about and remember for many a day to come.

For two days the house was full of gay folk, splendidly dressed, coming and going, talking and laughing. Then the King, laden with rich presents from the knight of Hinching-brooke, said good-bye, and rode away towards London.

Once more Oliver watched the grand procession, as it

splashed through the ford over the river Ouse and passed southward along the old Roman road, the Ermine Street. For one of the great roads which the Romans had made hundreds of years before runs right through Huntingdon.

These wise and wonderful people, when they tried to conquer Britain, knew that they must keep a way open to their ships. So, as they fought and chased the Britons from place to place, they made roads which seemed meant to last for ever, and over which their armies could easily pass. One of these roads led from the safe harbour of Southampton Water north-eastward to Huntingdon, then bent north-westward to the estuary of the Dee. Thus, cutting through forest, hill, and valley, the Romans joined two of the best harbourages in the island, and by this road their ships, lying safe in port, could easily be reached. In Southampton Water, Southampton, one of our greatest seaports, still lies. But the estuary of the Dee has long ago been silted up, and is now of little use for shipping.

Some people say that Ermine Street did not go westward to the Dee, but right northward to the Humber. In either case the road led from sea to sea and to safe harbourage. For the wise old Romans knew the value of a port which was as an open door, through which help might come, or escape might be made.

Chapter 2

SCHOOL DAYS

OLIVER had six sisters. He had brothers too, but they all died young, so I expect he grew up rather domineering. It is said that the year after the King visited Hinchingbrooke, his little son Prince Charles, then about four years old, came to spend a few days there, on his way to London. Oliver was sent for to play with the little Prince. But they did not get on at all well together. They soon began to quarrel, and then to fight. Oliver, who was bigger and a little older, gave Prince Charles such a blow between the eyes that it made his nose bleed. If the story is true, this was not a very good beginning, and, as you will see, these two little boys grew up to be deadly enemies.

When Oliver was old enough, he was sent to school. The school is still pointed out, although it, too, like the house in which he was born, has been built again. We do not know much about what Oliver did at school. Some old writers say he was a very naughty boy. He climbed trees, robbed orchards and dove-cots, and was always getting into mischief and danger. Once he fell into the river and was nearly drowned. But a clergyman, named Johnson, pulled him out. Many years after, when Oliver was marching through Huntingdon at the head of his rebel troops, he met this clergyman, then a very old man. Oliver knew him again. "Do you remember me?" he asked. "Once you saved my life."

"I do," replied the old man, "and I wish now that I had put you in rather than see you in arms against your King."

Some people say that Oliver did not learn much at school. Others say that he did. It seems at least that he was fond

OLIVER AND CHARLES.

of history and knew the stories of both Greek and Roman heroes. He liked Sir Walter Raleigh's "History of the World," too, and long years after advised his own son to read it. He also learned enough Latin to be able to talk it when he grew up and became a famous man.

Oliver was good at games. We do not know, but I think he must have played at soldiers with his school-fellows. I am sure that Oliver would always be general, and perhaps they marched along the Ermine Street and played at Romans and Britons. Perhaps, too, he sometimes sailed boats upon the lazy Great Ouse which flowed so slowly past his home.

Then his father might tell him how the river came winding and winding through the clay soil of Bedfordshire, at one place twisting about so much, that although it only got seventeen miles on its way, it wound about for forty-five. He might be told that the reason why the Great Ouse flowed slowly was because the land was so flat that it did not run down hill much to the sea. Then, too, he might know that the Great Ouse flowed into the Wash, where, he had learned in history, the bad King John was nearly drowned.

If you look at the map you will see that the Wash makes a big bend into the land. You will wonder why the clever Romans did not make their road go eastward to the Wash, for surely that big bay must be a good shelter for ships. But it is nothing of the kind. If you will look again at the map you will see that round the Wash there are no towns marked in big letters. That means that there are no large towns there. And the reason is that the Wash is quite useless for shipping. It is full of sand-banks, its low-lying coasts are damp and therefore foggy, the tide is rapid, and altogether it is one of the most dangerous places for ships on the east coast of England. The only part of the bay into which they may safely go lies along the Lincolnshire coast, and is called the Boston Deeps.

All these things and much besides Oliver would learn about his home and the places round it. At last he grew to be a big boy, and when he was seventeen years old it was decided to send him to college. So one fine morning, provided with every thing that befits a gentleman, he mounted upon his horse and rode away to Cambridge.

The country through which Oliver rode was little different from that which he had left. It was flat and swampy fen-land. In those days all the north of Cambridgeshire was little more than a watery desert. In the fens there were men called Fen-slodgers, who made a scanty living by catching the wild-fowl and the fish. These men were dreadfully poor, rough, ignorant, and half-savage. They walked about on high stilts, which both raised them out of the wet of the marshes and helped them to see their flocks of geese far across the fens. It was a miserable life, and, pale and gaunt, they prowled about the fens, shaking with ague, and bent with rheumatism, brought on by living in the constant damp.

Now all that is changed. Canals have been dug, dykes built, the water has been drained away, and Cambridgeshire has become one of the finest corn-growing counties of England. There is good pasture too, with dairy farms, where cheese is made which some people think as good as the famous cheese of Stilton.

So through fifteen miles of dreary fen-land Oliver rode until he came to the grey old town of Cambridge. Cambridge was then, as now, one of our two great University towns. It takes its name from the Cam, a tributary of the Great Ouse, upon which it lies.

There are seventeen colleges in Cambridge. The chief of them lie along the river bank, their still gardens and green, green lawns sloping to the water. The grey old buildings show calm and grand against the waving trees, and as one wanders

Halifax
YORK
Hull
Wakefield
Huddersfield
Humber
Spurn Hd.
Gt. Grimsby
Don
Trent
The Peak
Sheffield
Gainsborough
Mablethorpe
Buxton
Rother
Chesterfield
Lincoln
Horncastle
Winceby
LINCOLN
NORTH
SEA
DERBY
NOTTINGHAM
Leek
Southwell
Witham
Boston
Foulness
Dove
Nottingham
Boston Deeps
Fakenham
Derby
Trent
Grantham
The Wash
STAFFORD
Welland
The Fens
Lynn
G. Ouse
NORFOLK
Norwich
Lichfield
Ashby de la Zouche
RUTLAND
Oakham
Nen
Swaffham
Yarmouth
LEICESTER
Stamford
ISLE
Watton
Lowestoft
Birmingham
Market Bosworth
Leicester
OF
ELY
Attleborough
Waveney
Stilton
Ely
Coventry
Naseby
Kettering
HUNTINGDON
St. Ives
Halesworth
WORCESTER
NORTHAMPTON
Hinchinbrooke
Huntingdon
CAMBRIDGE
Newmarket
SUFFOLK
WARWICK
Holmby Ho.
St. Neots
Warwick
Daventry
Wellingborough
St. Neots
Ipswich
Avon
Northampton
Cambridge
Cam
Cropredy Br.
Bedford
Edge Hill
BEDFORD
Saffron Walden
Stour
The Naze
Banbury
Buntingford
Dunmow
Colchester
Blechington
BUCKINGHAM
HERTFORD
ESSEX
GLOUCESTER
OXFORD
Aylesbury
Islip
Berkhampstead
Hertford
R. Blackwater
Bampton
Oxford
St. Albans
Chelmsford
Isis
Abingdon
High Wycombe
Brentwood
Foulness I.
Faringdon
Uxbridge
Southend
Wooton Bassett
Henley
MIDDLESEX
Barking
Mouth of the Thames
LONDON
Woolwich
N. Foreland
BERKSHIRE
Windsor
Brentford
Greenwich
Sheppey I.
Reading
Egham
Staines
Blackheath
Newbury
Bagshot Heath
Hounslow
Rochester
WILTSHIRE
Woking
Canterbury
Ramsgate
Tidworth
Basingstoke
SURREY
Caterham
KENT
Andover
Guildford
Tonbridge
Dover
HAMPSHIRE
Wadhurst
Cranbrook
STRAIT OF DOVER
Calais
Salisbury
Winchester
Horsham
Uckfield
C. Gris Nez
Midhurst
SUSSEX
Battle
Hastings
Boulogne
Southampton
Portsmouth
Chichester
Brighton
Eastbourne
New Forest
Southampton
Spithead
Selsea Bill
Beachy Head
Hurst Cas.
Solent
Carisbrooke Cas.
DORSET
Avon
I. of Wight
Ventnor
FRANCE
ENGLISH CHANNEL
English Miles
10 5 0   10   20   30   40   50

among them to-day one is carried back to days long past. The University is so old that no one knows quite how old it is. Some Cambridge folk would like to think that it was founded by a Spaniard called Cantabar 375 years before Christ. But the oldest of the colleges now standing was not founded until the time of Edward I., although there was a school there long before, at which Henry Beauclerc, for one, was taught.

To Oliver, as he rode across the bridge over the Cam, the town must have seemed very beautiful and fresh, and he must have looked in wonder at the stately old buildings, for even in Cromwell's day many of the buildings were old. But it was to a new college that Cromwell went. It was Sidney-Sussex College. There he wrote his name in the list of scholars, "Oliver Cromwell from Huntingdon, admitted Fellow Commoner, 23rd April 1616."

Chapter 3

MAN'S ESTATE

OLIVER stayed little more than a year at Cambridge, for in the following June his father died, and once more he rode home to Huntingdon. Now he had to take his place as head of the house, and care for his mother and his sisters. But in those days, it was thought right that every country gentleman should know something of law. So once more Oliver put on his travelling dress, mounted his horse, and set out for London, there to study law. This was a much longer journey than he had taken before. We can imagine how excited the country boy—for he was little more—would be when he first rode into the great city, the capital of the kingdom.

London! To those of us who have seen it, what a picture the name calls up. Here are endless streets, miles upon miles of them, flanked by high houses, and pavements crowded with hundreds and thousands of people hurrying to and fro. In the roadway there is a thick and constant stream of cabs, carts, 'buses, grand carriages with prancing horses, little donkey-carts, unwieldy, noisy motors, and silent, swift electric cars. The air seems thick with sound, as the life of the great city hums and roars its way through the teeming streets.

The great broad river, too, which rolls under the many bridges on its way to the sea, is a busy thoroughfare. Up and down go mighty ships, clumsy barges, graceful little craft, laden with merchandise from all parts of the world. The banks are black with warehouses and noisy with shipbuilding. Everywhere there is clamour and bustle. It is a huge, busy, human hive, this London, the chief seaport in the kingdom, the richest and most populous city in all the world. And besides being the centre of trade, London is the seat of government, for there, in the stately halls at Westminster, Lords and Commons gather to make the laws by which the land shall be ruled.

London has grown to such importance and such greatness partly through its position. It lies upon the broad estuary of the Thames, on the eastern shores of Britain, making it easy to reach the European ports. The channel is safe, as the Wash is not, and wider and deeper than the Humber, although not deep enough for the great ships which are now built, so that many of them cannot come up to the port of London. It has one great fault as a port. It has no coal fields near, nor yet iron ore. These have to be brought a great distance, which makes them dear. So it is to be feared that some of the large shipbuilders will go away from the Thames to places nearer coal fields. Yet in spite of this fault, London has grown to be the heart of a vast network of road-, rail-, and water-ways, which lead out to all the world, and return again, carrying man and merchandise, as the veins and arteries carry blood to and from the heart of our body.

The London which Oliver looked upon was, of course, little like the London which we know. The streets were narrow and dirty, the houses mostly built of wood. Still it was a great and wonderful city. There mingled gay cavaliers, richly clad and decked with feathers and laces, sober Puritans, quaintly dressed soldiers, tradesmen, and merchants, a many-coloured crowd.

But again, of Oliver's life in this great city we know little. He made some friends, however—among them a certain Sir James Bourchier. This we know, for in 1620, when Oliver was twenty-one, he married Elizabeth, daughter of Sir James. The marriage took place at St. Giles's Church, Cripplegate. Then the young couple went home to Huntingdon.

There are people who say that Oliver was a naughty boy and a wild young man. Whether that be so or not, now at least he settled down quietly to farm the land which had been left him by his father. For the next ten years he lived a simple country life with his old mother and his good housewife Elizabeth.

While the years passed peacefully in Huntingdon, the King and his people had begun to quarrel. "The King can do no wrong," said James, and he tried to have all his own way. He tried, for one thing, to force every one to be of the same church—the English Church. But many did not like the English Church. It was too much like the Roman Catholic, which they hated. They wanted to do away with bishops, and robes and ceremonies, and have a very simple service. "No Bishop, no King," said James. And so the quarrel grew.

In 1625 James died, and his son Charles came to the throne. But with the new King things went no better. He wanted his own way quite as much as his father had done. So the quarrel between the King and people, between the King and Parliament, grew worse. Twice Charles called a Parliament. Twice, after a few weeks, he dissolved it in a passion, because the Commons would not vote him money unless he promised something in return. Then in 1628 he called a third Parliament. To this, as member for the town of Huntingdon, went Oliver Cromwell.

This was a remarkable Parliament. It passed an Act called the Petition of Right. This Act forbade the King to tax the people without first getting leave from Parliament. It forbade that men should be put in prison without a reason. It forbade that soldiers and sailors should be sent to live in people's houses, whenever and for as long a time as the King pleased. These were really no new laws. They were old ones, which the King had forgotten and broken. Charles, however, still went on taxing the people without leave, and the quarrel grew worse. Then the King ordered the Parliament to dissolve. At this the members were very angry, and as the Speaker tried to leave the hall, two of them held him down in his chair, crying, "He shall sit here till it please the House to rise."

There the Speaker was held, while the doors were locked, so that no man might go out and no man, not even the King's messenger, might come in. Then the Commons declared once more that it was against the law for the King to levy taxes without the consent of Parliament, and that any one paying such taxes was a traitor to the liberty of his country. For a few minutes the old hall rang with cheers. Then the members quickly scattered, for it was rumoured that soldiers were coming. That was the end of Parliament for the time, and Charles, finding that he could not make it do what he wanted, ruled without calling another for eleven years.

After taking part in these exciting doings Oliver went home, to settle down once more quietly to his farming.

Chapter 4.

THE LORD OF THE FENS

A year or two more passed quietly. Six children had now come to Oliver and Elizabeth. Their names were Robert, Oliver, Bridget, Richard, Henry, and Elizabeth.

Then, in 1631, Oliver made up his mind to sell his land in Huntingdon, and to go to St. Ives, a little town about five miles farther down the Great Ouse.

Except St. Neots, St. Ives is the only other town of any size in Huntingdonshire. In Saxon days, it was called Slepe, and under that name it is to be found in Doomsday Book. It is said to have received its new name from a Persian saint called Ivo, who came to England, died, and was buried at an old priory at Slepe about 600 A.D.

Oliver took a grazing farm on the lands of Slepe Hall, and began sheep-farming. Whether he ever lived in the house called Slepe Hall is not quite certain, but it used to be pointed out as his house. Many years ago it was pulled down, and now all that reminds us of him are the names Cromwell Place and Cromwell Terrace, which have been given to the houses built where Slepe Hall stood. But in many ways the town is still unchanged. Across the river there is a bridge over which Oliver must often have tramped in his heavy boots. It has a quaint, old-world air about it, reminding us of other times, and on the middle of it stands a house once used, it is thought, as a lighthouse.

When Oliver went to St. Ives he had grown into a sad, stern man. Perhaps the dreary country in which he lived had something to do with making him so. Certainly the time in which he lived had. Often he was seized with fits of gloom. He felt that, in the eyes of God, he was a great sinner. Then he would pray in deep trouble of soul. And so, as with fire and with hammer, religion was wrought into his life, and at last he found comfort and calm of spirit.

Oliver looked darkly on the ceremony and service of the Church of England. Yet still he went to church like other people, often, we are told, wearing a piece of red flannel round his neck, as his throat was weak. All his children were baptized too in the church, as other children were.

Oliver would have none but godly men to work for him. Before they went to work he gathered them for prayers; indeed one old writer says that he kept them so long at prayer that they had no time to do their proper work, and that therefore the farm did not prosper.

However that may be, Oliver soon left St. Ives, and went to the cathedral town of Ely. Ely, like St. Ives, is upon the Great Ouse, but it is in Cambridgeshire, not in Huntingdonshire.

Oliver moved to Ely because his uncle, Sir Thomas Stewart, his mother's brother, died and left him money and lands there. The house in which he lived in Ely was then called the Glebe House, and may still be seen.

Ely is a city, yet, save for its cathedral, it looks more like a village, and, unlike any other English city, it sends no member to Parliament. Great numbers of eels used to be found in the waters round, and from that the city takes its name. It is built upon the Isle of Ely, which, before the fens were drained, was really an island rising above the surrounding marsh-land. In summer the city could only be reached by certain roads through the fens. In winter it was quite surrounded by water so deep that boats could sail upon it. Even yet the country looks dreary and deserted in winter, but in summer it is a waving plain of golden corn-fields, and out of it, seen from far, a landmark to all the fen country, rise the towers of the great cathedral.

From very early times there has been a monastery at Ely,

but the oldest part of the present cathedral was built after William the Conqueror came. It was a spot loved by Canute the Dane. Here one winter's day, when the fens were frozen, Budde the Stout, a bondman, crossed the ice before Canute, to try with his great weight if it were strong enough to bear the King. And as a reward for this brave service Budde received his freedom.

When William of Normandy came it was in the Isle of Ely that Englishmen made their last stand against the Conqueror. For the marsh-lands around made it a natural fortress, and it needed both the great William's "land force and ship force" to dislodge them. And so on through all our history Ely plays a part—in the civil war between Matilda and Stephen, in the Barons' War, in the time of Henry III.—and now it gave to Cromwell the title of "Lord of the Fens."

The King, needing money, was hard put to it, and invented many ways to get it. He ordered, for one thing, that London should grow no larger. He fined those who built new houses, and he pulled down some, fining the owners for not having done so sooner. It seemed to him now that some money might be made by draining the fens, and a clever Flemish engineer, called Vermuyden, had already begun the work. But the fen-slodgers cried out against it. If the fens were drained the scanty living which they earned by fishing and fowling would be gone. Others, too, joined the cry. It was but a new trick of the King, they said, to get money without the people's aid, and so to continue to rule without Parliament.

Oliver Cromwell, too, had a word to say. And he said and did with so much force that the drainage works were given up. Then the people whose part he had taken against the King gave him a new name. They called him "Lord of the Fens." Yet later, when it was no longer a question of the

King, but only of the good of the people, Oliver helped on the drainage with all his might. It was not, however, until the nineteenth century that the great work was finished by the engineers Rennie and Telford. It had taken three hundred years to turn a dreary waste of marsh into fertile, smiling plains.

Chapter 5

THE GATHERING STORM

KING Charles went blindly on his way. Aided by Laud and Strafford, he thought to make the people bow to his will. "Be a King like the King of France," said his French wife. But Englishmen and Scotsmen he found were stiff-necked and hard to bend. Then at last, the Scots, goaded into rebellion, took up arms against their King. The rattle of sword and musket, the tramp of many feet marching in time, the shout of the drill-sergeant, were heard in every town and village, as men gathered to fight for their liberty and their religion. "For Christ's Crown and Covenant" was the motto which fluttered before the tent of each captain, as he lay encamped upon Duns Law.

With an empty purse it was an ill matter for the King to gather men. But by desperate effort he did collect an army of a kind, and marched against the Scots. The men on the King's side, however, had no heart in the matter. There was no fighting. Charles gave way, and marched back to England a sorely angry man.

Then, still bent on punishing the Scots, Charles called a Parliament. It was a case of needs must. For to fight the Scots the King must have money, and he hoped that now the Commons would be more willing to grant him what he asked.

To this Parliament went Oliver, as member for Cambridge. He had now grown into a grave, stern farmer of forty, a man hating Popery, loving his country, fearing God, carrying his Bible in his hand and the words of it in his heart and on his tongue, a man of strong action and fierce passion, not always held in check. We know what he looked like at this time, for a young Cavalier, hearing him speak in Parliament, wrote of him as he saw him. "He was dressed," he says, "in a plain cloth suit, which seemed to have been made by an ill country-tailor. His linen was plain and not very clean. And I remember a speck or two of blood upon his little band, which was not much larger than his collar. His hat was without a hat-band. His stature was of good size, his sword stuck close to his side; his countenance swollen and reddish, his voice sharp and untuneable, and his eloquence full of fervour." Such a man was Oliver in 1640, when, after ruling eleven years without one, King Charles again called a Parliament.

But the men of England were no more easily moved than they had been eleven years before. Not a penny would they vote their King. "Till the liberties of the House and of the kingdom are cleared, we know not whether we have anything to give or no," they said.

Then, in hot anger, the King dissolved Parliament once more. It had sat only for three weeks, and is known as the Short Parliament.

Again, with a mighty effort, the King raised an army, and sent it marching northward. But now the Scots marched into England to meet it, and, for almost the first time in history, they were greeted by the English as friends, not foes.

But there was no more heart in the King's army than there had been the year before. It was a Bishops' War, the soldiers said, and they had no liking for bishops. The Scots had the best of the little fighting there was, and from York the King turned back to London to call another Parliament. This was the famous Long Parliament. It first met on 23rd November 1640. Again Oliver sat as member for Cambridge.

One of the first things which the new Parliament did was to seize and imprison Lord Strafford and Archbishop Laud. They had been evil advisers to the King, they said. Strafford was condemned to death and executed. Laud remained in prison for four years. Then he too went to his death.

Charles could not save his friends. He could as little save himself. The Commons would by no means do as he wished, so he made up his mind to seize five of them whom he thought were his worst enemies. In this the Queen encouraged him. "Go, you coward," she said, "and pull these rogues out by the ears."

So Charles, with three hundred soldiers behind him, marched down to the House. Leaving his men without, Charles himself strode into the Hall. Going right up to the chair, "Mr. Speaker," he said, "by your leave I must borrow your chair for a little."

The Speaker rising, fell upon his knees, and as Charles seated himself the members too rose, and stood bare-headed before their King.

With keen, sharp eyes Charles looked round the House. Not one of the five members was to be seen. They had been warned, and had fled.

"Mr. Speaker," said the King at length, "are any of these five members here? Do you see any of them? Where are they?"

The Speaker, who had stood up, now again fell upon his knees. "Your Majesty," he said, "I have neither eyes to see, nor tongue to speak, in this place, save as the House is pleased to direct me."

"It matters not. I think mine eyes are as good as any," replied Charles. Once more he looked keenly round. Then he said, "Ah, I see the birds are flown." And in bitter anger the baffled King left the House, followed by loud cries of rage from the members.

The King had trampled on their ancient rights and freedom. Where would it end?

Chapter 6.

THE STORM BREAKS

A few days after his ill-fated visit to the House of Parliament, Charles left Whitehall and London. He was never to come there again until he came as a prisoner. The storm was darkening down. The Queen fled to Holland, secretly taking with her the crown jewels, to pawn them in order to get money for the King.

When the Queen had gone, Charles travelled northward. Full of thoughts of war, he meant to take possession of Hull. First, because there were stored the arms which had been gathered for the Scots war. Second, because it was the most convenient port at which soldiers from the Continent might land—soldiers whom the Queen was to hire to fight against the English with the money got by pawning the English crown jewels.

Hull, or, as the full name is, Kingston-on-Hull, lies on the north side of the Humber. It was the great English King, Edward I., who gave it the name of Kingstown or Kingston. One day while he was out hunting he came upon the little village of Wyke, as it was called. His quick eye and mind saw at once how well the place was fitted for a seaport. So he made it a free town, gave it many privileges, and encouraged people to live there. Soon it grew to be a busy port. To-day, if you wander among the docks, you will see all sorts of merchandise piled upon the quays. You will see wool from Germany and Australia on its way to the cloth mills of Yorkshire, iron bars from Sweden for Sheffield, or you may see bales of finished woollen goods and cases of cutlery coming back from the mills and workshops, ready to be carried to all parts of the world. You will also see great lines of coal trains, for Hull is the outlet for the coal mines of Yorkshire, from which thousands of tons are exported every year. These coal fields are so large that it is thought that they will last seven hundred years longer, even if they are worked as fast as they are at present.

But in the days of King Charles, Hull had not grown to be the great town it now is. Instead of being the fifth seaport in the kingdom, instead of its miles of docks and shipbuilding yards, it had but one harbour at the mouth of the little river Hull upon which it lies. But it was a safe harbour. Coming from Holland, troops might sail up the Humber, land at Hull, and soon be in the very heart of the country.

Between the Thames and the Humber there is no other opening on the east coast—the Wash, you know, is of no use. Charles knew he could not command London. There the rebel Parliament was supreme. Hull he must have.

So, one day, the Governor of Hull was told that the King, with three hundred armed followers, was marching on the town. The Governor sent a message to the King praying him not to come. But the King would not listen; he still came on. Then the Governor drew up the bridge and shut the gates against him.

When the King came to the walls he found the town ready as if to receive an enemy. He called upon the Governor and commanded him to open the gates. Then the Governor came to the wall and fell upon his knees before the King, swearing that he was his faithful subject. Yet he would not open the gate, nor let the King enter.

"I dare not," he said, "being trusted by the Parliament."

For four hours the King stood without. Many messages passed all in vain, and at length, weary and angry, Charles bade the heralds proclaim the Governor to be a traitor. Then he turned and rode away.

So at last the storm broke, war began, and all the country took sides, some for the King, some for Parliament. To some it was a war of civil and political freedom. That is, to them it meant settling the question whether the King should have the power of forcing the people to pay taxes when he liked without the consent of Parliament. To others it was a war of religious freedom. That is, to them it meant settling the question whether the King should have the power of forcing his people to worship God in a way which they did not think to be right. And so it came about that the paying of taxes and the worshipping of God became strangely mixed up in men's minds.

It was a very dreadful war which now began. Families were divided, brother fighting against brother, father against son. Friends who had been dear to each other took different sides, and so became bitter enemies. Yet on the whole England might be said to be cut in two, the east fighting for Parliament, the north and west for the King. Where rich and busy towns had sprung up, along the river banks like the Humber and Thames, where people had made money by trading with foreign countries, there the anger against the King's unlawful taxes was hottest. These took sides with the Parliament. But most of the lords and gentlemen were for the King. So it was from the inland, rural districts, where the people were farmers and tillers of the ground, renting their lands from the nobles, that the followers of the King came; and from the Universities and the cathedral cities, where the bishops held sway. For the most part it was the merchants and traders, the artisans and mechanics, who were for the Parliament, and the gentlemen, their followers and servants, who were for the King.

So you see that the geography of England had something to do with the sides which people took in this great struggle.

The navy declared for Parliament, for the King had made

the sailors angry by calling them "water rats." So most of the seaports fell into their hands. Thus from the beginning Parliament had some advantages. Having command of the sea-ports they were able to seize all the ships and men which came from abroad to help the King. They had also far more money than the King, as most of the merchants and traders were on their side. And it is in the hands of its merchants that the greatest wealth of a country lies.

Chapter 7

THE THIMBLE AND BODKIN ARMY

THE King now began to gather an army. One blustering August day he set up his standard at Nottingham, calling on all true men to rally to the defence of their King and country. The standard made a very grand show. It had many streamers, and at the top was a white flag, bearing the arms of the King, a hand pointing to the crown, and a motto, "Give Cæsar his due." With beat of drum and blare of trumpet it was set up. But so wild was the wind that soon the gay streamers and white flag were trailing in the dust. This seemed an evil omen to the King's friends, and, as the wind still blew fiercely, it was some days before the standard could be set up again.

In London, the Parliament too was gathering an army. Every one was eager to help. Those who could not fight brought money and jewels. Women who had nothing else to give brought their silver thimbles and bodkins, so that the Cavaliers, as the King's friends were called, named it, in scorn, "the thimble and bodkin army."

Oliver Cromwell was among those most eager to help. He gave £500, besides £100 worth of arms, for the men of Cambridge, whom he began to drill. He was made a captain, and one of the first things which we find him doing is stopping the King's soldiers who had been sent to seize, for the King's use, the valuable gold and silver plate belonging to the University of Cambridge. Instead of letting the King have it, Cromwell seized it himself for the Parliament, thereby winning for them about £20,000. This was a great service, for in war money is one of the most needful things.

Although most of the nobles were on the King's side, a few

were on the side of the Parliament. Among those was Robert, Earl of Essex. He was made commander of part of the army. The Earl of Manchester was made commander of another part.

The King's commander was the Earl of Lindsay, and Prince Rupert, the King's dashing nephew, was his commander of horse.

At first the Royalist army was small, and, besides being few in number, the soldiers were badly armed. Some of them had nothing but sticks to fight with. Those who had muskets had no swords. The pikemen had no breast-plates, which were still used, although, since gunpowder had been invented, armour was worn less and less.

The Parliamentarians, on the other hand, having command both of London and of Hull, where great war stores were gathered, were well armed. But many of them did not know how to use their weapons and had never fought before. Nor did Essex make good use of his advantage. Instead of fighting at once, as long as the King's army was small, he waited until many faithful men had gathered to him.

From Nottingham Charles moved to Shrewsbury. Then, as Essex still lay idle, he made up his mind to march on London, and once more gain possession of the capital. At last, seeing what the King meant to do, Essex was roused. Hurriedly leaving his camp at Worcester, he marched after the King. The King turned, and, at Edgehill, in Warwickshire, the two armies met. There the first real battle of the war was fought.

The King's army numbered about 14,000 men, the Parliamentarian only about 10,000, for Essex had marched so quickly that many of his soldiers were left behind, under another great general, called Hampden.

Upon the slopes of Edgehill the King took his stand. Below, in the Vale of the Red Horse, were the Parliamentarians. The valley was so called from a horse which was cut in the turf

RUPERT'S CHARGE AT EDGEHILL.

upon the hill-side, showing the red sandstone with which so much of Warwickshire is covered.

There, from early morning till about two in the afternoon, lay the two armies in the still sunshine of an October Sunday, neither side firing a shot or advancing a step. The King would not leave his safe position. Essex would not charge uphill. Neither side was willing, perhaps, to be the first to break the peace, and spill a brother's blood.

Along the lines of the Parliamentarians rode ministers, preaching and praying, and the sound of psalm-singing broke the Sabbath calm.

The King on his side galloped among his men, speaking brave words to them. Over his steel armour, which flashed in the sunlight, he wore a black velvet cloak. On his breast sparkled the star and George of the Order of the Garter.

At length, weary of waiting, Essex gave the order to fire. For an hour the great cannon spoke and answered, awaking the silence of vale and hill. Then the King's lines advanced. Dashing Prince Rupert would have it so. Cautious Lindsay shook his head and gave the word. "O Lord," he prayed, "Thou knowest how busy I must be this day; if I forget Thee, do not Thou forget me. March on, boys."

Like a whirlwind Prince Rupert dashed upon and broke through the Parliamentarian line, scattering and chasing them to the village of Kineton, three miles beyond, leaving the Vale of the Horse red in his tracks. But at Kineton he stayed to plunder, and meanwhile things went ill with the King. Lindsay was wounded to death. The royal standard was lost, but recovered again. At last night fell and put an end to the strife.

On both sides there had been great deeds of valour. On both sides there had been bad mistakes, friend sometimes firing upon friend. On both sides many had fled. Not a few shopmen and artisans in "the thimble and bodkin army" were new to the use of sword and pike, new to the flash and roar of cannon, yet, if some among them fled, others stood to their posts, among them Captain Oliver Cromwell and his horsemen.

Both sides claimed the victory. But both sides had lost many men, and although at day-break Hampden came up with his fresh troops, Essex was too down-hearted to fight again. So he fell back upon Warwick.

The King marched forward, took Banbury without a blow, and from there went on his way towards London. At Oxford, which he made his headquarters for the rest of the war, he halted.

Chapter 8

THE KING AT OXFORD

OXFORD, like London, is upon the Thames. But how different in every way the two towns are! In London, the streets are full of hurrying throngs, and all day long the beat of feet and roar of traffic fills the air. The river, crowded with ships, both great and small, flows dark and muddy. The banks, lined with warehouses, are noisy and busy with trade and shipbuilding.

At Oxford it is very different. The river even has changed its name and is here called the Isis. It flows between green meadows starred with flowers and shadowed with leafy trees, and on its clear waters, though there is scarce a sail, there is many a punt and canoe, and by the bank a gay line of college barges.

Beyond the trees rise the old grey colleges, dim and weather-worn with the storms and sunshine of many a hundred years, beautiful with tower and turret, and tracery of stone-work. Here there is neither bustle nor din. Peacefully Oxford lies as if sleeping in the sunlight, but within these old grey walls are gathered treasures of learning from past ages. Through the silent courtyards many a famous and learned man has trod, down the peaceful streets have passed many a fair lady and gallant knight.

Oxford, like Cambridge, claims to be very ancient. One old writer says that the city was built more than 1000 years B.C., and that it took its name, Oxford, from old British words meaning the ford for oxen. Another thinks the University was founded by some Greeks who came with Brutus of Troy—that Brutus who changed the name of Albion to Britain. But these are fairy tales. Certain it is Oxford has played a part many a time in our history. Before the Conquest the Witenagemot was sometimes held there. The soldiers of Stephen besieged it, and from it Queen Matilda fled away over the frozen snow. There was held the "Mad Parliament," when, for the first time since the Conquest, English laws were written again in English. And now, in the Great Civil War, it was to be the scene of gaiety and laughter, of blood and battle.

Soon the grey old courtyards were awakened with song and laughter. For the court of Charles was gay even in this time of bitterness and war. Fair ladies and fine gentlemen stepped about the green lawns, mingling strangely with grave professors and noisy students. Here the Queen rejoined her husband, and here too the King held his Parliament—the "Mongrel Parliament," as Charles himself called it. It was made up of those nobles and gentlemen who had left the Puritan Parliament in London, or who had been cast out of it. But the Mongrel Parliament was of little use, and Charles soon dissolved it, as he had dissolved so many others.

Meanwhile Prince Rupert, or "Prince Robber," as the people learned to call him, scoured the country round, robbing and plundering. To Abingdon, Henley, Egham, Staines, Hounslow, Brentford, nearer and nearer to London he came, followed by the King and all the royal army. The shopkeepers and merchants of London had dug trenches and built walls around the city to keep it safe, and now they marched out under Essex, and camped upon Turnham Green, ready to defend their homes. They were 24,000 strong, and a skilful general might easily have surrounded the King's army and cut off his retreat to Oxford. But Essex was slow and hesitating. He gave orders and recalled them again. He acted indeed as if he were afraid of beating the King too thoroughly, and so Charles got safely back to Oxford. There were men who grumbled and said that Essex was no true Parliamentarian, yet, when later, the King tried to bribe him back to his side, the old general would not listen.

But Captain Oliver Cromwell watched all these things, thinking his own thoughts. After Edgehill he had spoken wise words to his friend John Hampden. "Your troops," he said, "are old, decayed serving-men and tapsters, and such kind of fellows. Their troops" (meaning the Royalist troops) "are gentlemen's sons, younger sons, and persons of quality. Do you think that the spirits of such base and mean fellows will ever be able to encounter gentlemen, and have honour, and courage and resolution in them? You must get men of a spirit that is likely to go on as far as gentlemen will go—or else you will be beaten still."

And John Hampden, a wise and gallant man, and a true patriot, thought that Oliver talked indeed good sense but of what was not possible.

But when Oliver spoke of "gentlemen," he did not mean fine clothes and grand manners. He meant men, brave and good. "A few honest men are better than numbers," he said. "If you choose godly, honest men to be captains of horse, honest men will follow them. I had rather have a plain russet-coated captain that knows what he fights for, and loves what he knows, that what you call a 'gentleman' and is nothing else. I honour a *Gentleman* that is so indeed."

So, while Essex hesitated and debated, Captain Cromwell worked in his own county, doing what he could. He rode here, there, and everywhere, fighting and drilling, talking and writing letters, increasing his troops until he had nearly 1000 men—"a lovely company," as he himself calls them, "honest, sober Christians, who expect to be used as men."

Chapter 9.
COLONEL CROMWELL

THERE is no room in this little book to follow all the sieges and battles of the war, or even all those in which Oliver took part. He did not long remain a captain, but was soon made a colonel. He was a great soldier, and his movements were rapid. We find him at Cambridge, Norwich, Lowestoft, Lynn, back again at Cambridge, then marching into Huntingdonshire to quell the "malignants" there, searching even in the house of his old uncle, who was still a Royalist, for war stores.

Next he is at Peterborough, stabling his horses in the cathedral nave, for was he not doing God's work, and might not His house give shelter to His servants? Then on to Stamford, on the borders of Northampton, Rutland, and Lincolnshire. Into Lincolnshire itself, now a very stronghold of the Royalists, at Grantham and Gainsborough we find him. Three days after a victorious fight at the last-named place, he is back again in Huntingdon, working to raise more men and money. "Out instantly, all of you!" he writes. "Raise your bands: send them to Huntingdon; get up what volunteers you can; hasten your horse. You must act lively! Neglect no means!" Then northward again he goes to Boston, impetuous as Prince Robber, yet cool and calm, striking or staying his hand when need be. Next he is at Horncastle, and at Winceby, a few miles off, with other Parliamentarians, routs the Royalists utterly. So little by little Lincolnshire was won for the Parliament.

But if Lincolnshire and the eastern counties—Cambridge, Norfolk, Suffolk, Essex, Hertfordshire, and Huntingdon—stood for the Parliament, in Yorkshire and the west the King held his own.

The town of Bristol had fallen to him, and Gloucester had been with difficulty saved. Indeed, when the year 1643 closed, it seemed as if the King had had the best of the war. Here, there, everywhere, through all the country the fires of battle blazed. Towns were taken and retaken, now held for the King, now for the Parliament. Amid the rain of winter, under the sunshine of early spring, in the standing corn of autumn, battles were fought. The people grew weary of a war which dragged on month after month and seemed no nearer an end.

The Scots beyond the border watched the fight sway this way and that. The English Parliament had now much need of help. So these two ancient enemies, Englishmen and Scotsmen, swore together a Solemn League and Covenant. They bound themselves to be all of one church, the Presbyterian Church, and bishops were to be no more. They swore to preserve the laws of the land and the liberties of the people. Then in January 1644 a Scots army, under Alexander Leslie, Earl of Leven, came marching across the border, over the frozen Tweed, to the aid of their English brethren.

As the Scots advanced, the tide of war set northward, till it closed around the city of York, where the Royalists lay besieged.

Where the Ouse—not the Great Ouse which Cromwell knew so well, but the Yorkshire Ouse—begins to be navigable, where the three divisions of Yorkshire called the Ridings join, on the direct road to Scotland, in the centre of the great plain of York lies the northern capital, as it may be named.

York was a great city even in the days of the Romans, being the seat of government when London was but a trading port. Here Severus died, and Constantine. Here Constantine the Great was proclaimed Emperor. In Saxon times York became a centre of learning and piety. Here Edwin, King of Northumbria, was baptized on Easter Day, 627, and founded

Berwick
Tweed
SCOTLAND
Cheviot Hills
Alnwick
NORTHUMBERLAND
Nith
NORTH
Newcastle
Tyne
SEA
Solway Firth
Carlisle
Pennine
Durham
CUMBERLAND
Wear
DURHAM
WESTMORLAND
Tees
Cleveland
Swale
Moors
Furness
Kirkby
Lonsdale
Chain
Northallerton
Barrow
Y O R K
Wolds
IRISH
Knaresborough
York
Skipton
SEA
Gisburne
Marston Moor
Stamford Br.
Stonyhurst
Ribble
Towton
Ouse
Hull
Preston Moor
Aire
Hull
Preston
Halifax
LANCASHIRE
Barnsley
Wigan
Manchester
Trent
Liverpool
Winwick
Sheffield
Gainsborough
Warrington
Mersey
LINCOLN
Dee
CHESHIRE
DERBY
DENBIGH FLINT
NOTTINGHAM
Horncastle
Winceby
English Miles
0   10   20   30   40   50   60

the church which stood where the great Minster now stands. York is the seat of one of the two archbishoprics of England, and the Minster might be said to be the heart of Yorkshire.

Yorkshire is the largest county in England, and has also more people in it than any other county. Yet it is really all the basin of one great river—the Ouse. The great plain of York runs right through the centre, from north to south. On either side are highlands, the Pennine range on the west, the Yorkshire and Cleveland moors and the Yorkshire Wolds on the east. On the slopes of the Pennines, where the pasture is good, there are many sheep farms. Because of the wool and because of the water-power coming from the streams of the Pennine slopes, people built cloth mills there. Thus many manufacturing towns have sprung up. Other towns have grown because of the coal and iron fields, Sheffield having become famous all the world over for its steel goods. And the trade of all these Yorkshire towns passing through Hull makes it, as you know, great too.

The plain of York is rich and fertile, and there much wheat is grown, and all about are scattered prosperous little agricultural towns. Yet York itself has never become great in trade. It is the ecclesiastical capital, and, with its old walls and grand Minster, seems to be a link between the busy present and the grey old past.

Chapter 10

IRONSIDES

UPON the plain of York, forming as it does a natural battle-field, some of the fiercest battles of English history have been fought. Here, at Stamford Bridge, Harold of England fought and defeated Harold of Norway, before he hurried southward to meet the great Duke William. Here, at Towton, amid a blinding snowstorm, was fought one of the deadliest battles of the Roses, the bloodiest battle fought on English ground since Hastings. And now in 1644, on Marston Moor, again in civil war, the forces of the King and people faced each other—Scots and Puritans against Cavaliers.

All through a thunderous July day the troops on either side lay waiting, marching or deploying. Scorched with the burning sun, soaked with sudden blasts of stormy rain, yet firing no shot, they waited, the Parliamentarians singing psalms meantime among the trampled corn.

About two o'clock some guns were fired, and until five from time to time shot answered shot, but neither side advanced. At five, a stillness and deep silence fell upon the waiting armies. There would be no fighting that day, said the Cavaliers, as it neared seven in the evening. Then suddenly the signal was given. "God and the King!" cried one side. "God with us!" replied the other.

The thunders of war were loose. A shot grazed Cromwell's neck, drawing blood. "A miss is as good as a mile," he laughed, and charged with his men.

"Lieutenant-General Cromwell's own division had a handful of it, for they were charged by Rupert's bravest men, both in front and flanks," writes one who saw them. "They stood at the sword point a pretty while hacking one another. But at last it pleased God he brake through them, and scattered them before him like a dust."

Like dust the dashing Prince of Plunderers and his men fled before the Ironsides. For it was at this battle that they first got the name by which they became famous, and it was Prince Rupert himself who gave it to them, or rather, he called Cromwell himself Ironsides, and the name afterwards was given to his men too.

But while Rupert fled before Cromwell, in the rest of the field things went ill with the Parliament, and Cromwell, returning from the chase in the waning light of the summer evening, found the battle all but lost. Again he charged, and, backed by the Scots under General David Leslie, turned defeat into victory. "God made them as stubble to our swords," he said.

The sun had set, and the pale moon shone calmly on the ghastly scene ere the slaughter and the chase were over. From Marston Moor all the way to York, the road was marked by a red line of dead and dying. Of the four thousand and more who lay there, turning their pale faces and unseeing eyes to the starry sky, three thousand were men who had fought and died for their King.

After the battle of Marston Moor, the Parliamentarians again besieged York, which soon yielded to them. The Royalists who had so gallantly defended it were allowed to march out with all the honours of war. And with colours flying and drums beating, making a brave show, they went, while their grave foes thronged the Minster, singing psalms of praise and victory.

Then the Scots, marching northward, took Newcastle, the only port left to the King.

Newcastle-on-Tyne takes its name from the "new castle" which William the Conqueror built there. It was a town well known to the Scots. For lying, as it does, so near the border, it had been besieged many a time by them during their almost constant wars with the English. Parts of the old walls of the town may still be seen, for they were built strong and high, so that people might sleep safe and not fear to be dragged out of their beds by Scotch marauders. The houses, too, were strongly built, for an old writer says: "The vicinity of the Scots made them to build not for state but strength."

The county of Northumberland, in which Newcastle lies, is for a great part nothing but hill and moor. On the north are the Cheviots, and on the west the Pennines. The moors running down from these hills are very bleak and lonely. They are swept by cold mist-laden winds. Few people live there, and only sheep are reared upon the bare hill-sides.

But Newcastle itself is a busy, smoky seaport. It stands upon the most famous coal field in the world, and exports more coal than any town in Great Britain except Cardiff. It is from this coal that the county gets its wealth. "To carry coals to Newcastle"—meaning, to give oneself needless trouble—had already passed into a proverb more than three hundred years ago. And besides being on a coal field, Newcastle is near lead and iron mines. It is upon a navigable river, the Tyne, which, rising in the Pennines, flows right through the coal district to the sea. So it is little wonder that Newcastle has grown into a vast workshop.

Here in the Armstrong works ironclads are built, cannon and guns are cast. In the Stephenson works, which take their name from the famous engineer George Stephenson, locomotives and heavy machinery of all kinds are made. Here there are shot works, glass works, lead-smelting works, and so on through an endless list of manufactories. From Newcastle to the sea the river banks seem one great factory. By day the air is dark with smoke and steam, and noisy with the ring of a thousand hammers. By night the flare of a hundred fires reddens the sky for miles around. And up and down the river vessels big and little sail ceaselessly, bringing and taking away merchandise.

But in the time of Charles the town of Newcastle was by no means so great, nor the port so good as it is now. The channel was narrow and across it lay a bar of sand, where at low tide there was scarcely six feet of water. Still, it was the only port looking towards the Continent which the King had been able to keep, and the loss of it was a bitter blow.

Now, with great labour and expense, the channel has been deepened and the bar removed, so that the largest vessels can safely go where once quite small ones would have grounded, and over the bar instead of six there are twenty-five feet of water. This has been done by the Tyne Improvement Commissioners, that the town might keep pace with its growing trade.

Chapter 11

THE SELF-DENYING ORDINANCE

AFTER the taking of Newcastle, all the North, it might be said, was in the hands of the Parliamentarians. But elsewhere the King was victorious. He defeated General William Waller, once fondly nick-named "William the Conqueror," at Cropredy Bridge, in Oxfordshire. In Cornwall, the Earl of Essex fled before him. In the North, the Earl of Manchester, under whom Cromwell now served, was slow to move. Cromwell, indignant and impatient, chafed as one of his own horses might have done at a restraining bit. In vain he argued and advised. Manchester moved so slowly that the King reached his headquarters at Oxford once more in safety.

Then leaving the battle-field, we find Cromwell back in his old place in Parliament, as member for Cambridge.

We can imagine him striding across the floor, stamping to his seat in his great riding-boots. His face is ruddy, and bronzed with sun and wind, his dress more slovenly than ever, perhaps with more spots of blood upon it. And there in his voice, "sharp and untuneable" as of old, he lays grave charges at the door of my lord of Manchester. Since the taking of York he had acted as if he had done enough, refusing to fight on one pretence or another; delaying and offputting as if he feared to bring the King too low.

With words as bitter Lord Manchester replied. For had not this loud-voiced soldier declared that there would be no good days in England until they had done with lords, until my lord himself was but plain "Mr. Montague"? Had he not said that if he met the King in battle, he would fire his pistol at him as soon as at any man? Had he not also openly scoffed at the Solemn League and Covenant and the compact with the Scots?

But Cromwell was not to be silenced. "It is now a time to speak or for ever hold the tongue," he said. And speak he would, "To save the nation out of a bleeding, nay, a dying state," else, "we shall make the kingdom weary of us, and hate the name of Parliament."

Already the Puritan Parliament was divided into two parties, the Presbyterian and the Independent. The Presbyterians were those who clung to a strict and narrow form of worship, and who could see no good in any man who did not think as they, and love the Solemn League and Covenant as they did. The Independents, of whom Cromwell was one of the greatest, while hating the Episcopalians as truly as the Presbyterians, yet did not love the Covenant, and claimed a greater freedom in religion. "The State," said Cromwell, "in choosing men to serve it, takes no notice of their opinions; if they be willing faithfully to serve it,—that satisfies." "Take heed of being sharp against those to whom you can object little but that they square not with you in every opinion concerning matters of religion."

And although, later, Parliament came to disagree with Cromwell on many matters, at this time, most of the Commons saw that he was right, and that, if they were to succeed and at last bring the country to peace, something must be done. "Whatever the cause," said another member, "two summers are passed over, and we are not saved. Our victories seem to have been put into a bag with holes. What we won one time we lost another. A summer's victory has proved but a winter's story. Men's hearts have failed them with the seeing of these things."

One reason for these empty victories and heavy losses was that the army of the Parliament, instead of being under only one leader was under many—Essex, Manchester, Waller, Fairfax, and others. These generals did not work together, they did not help nor understand each other, and so came troubles and difficulties.

Another member now proposed that no member of Parliament, whether of Lords or Commons, should hold any Government post, either as an officer in the army or in any other way. This he proposed, so that men like Essex, Manchester, Waller, and others, who had proved themselves to be poor generals, should be obliged to lay down their command. Then the Parliament would be free to choose what leaders they liked.

At first the lords would not hear of this proposal. The nobles had always been leaders of the army, and they wished still to remain so; but after some time they gave way, and the famous Act, called the Self-Denying Ordinance, was passed. By this, every officer who was a member of Parliament was obliged to give up his command within forty days.

Then the army was remodeled and placed under one commander-in-chief. For this post Sir Thomas Fairfax was chosen. He was only thirty-three, but he had been in many battles, and his face was scarred with wounds. He was tall and dark, very quiet in peace, but like a lion in the field, dashing yet decided. "Black Tom" his men called him.

An old and clever soldier, Sir Philip Skippon, was made the new commander's major-general. But the post of lieutenant-general was left empty. This could scarcely be by accident.

But already, having said his say, before the passing of the Self-Denying Ordinance, Oliver Cromwell had galloped off to the battle-field once more. In the west, at Weymouth, Taunton, and Salisbury, we find him. True, according to the new Act, he was no longer an officer. But the King was in the field again, some one must be sent to face him, and Fairfax,

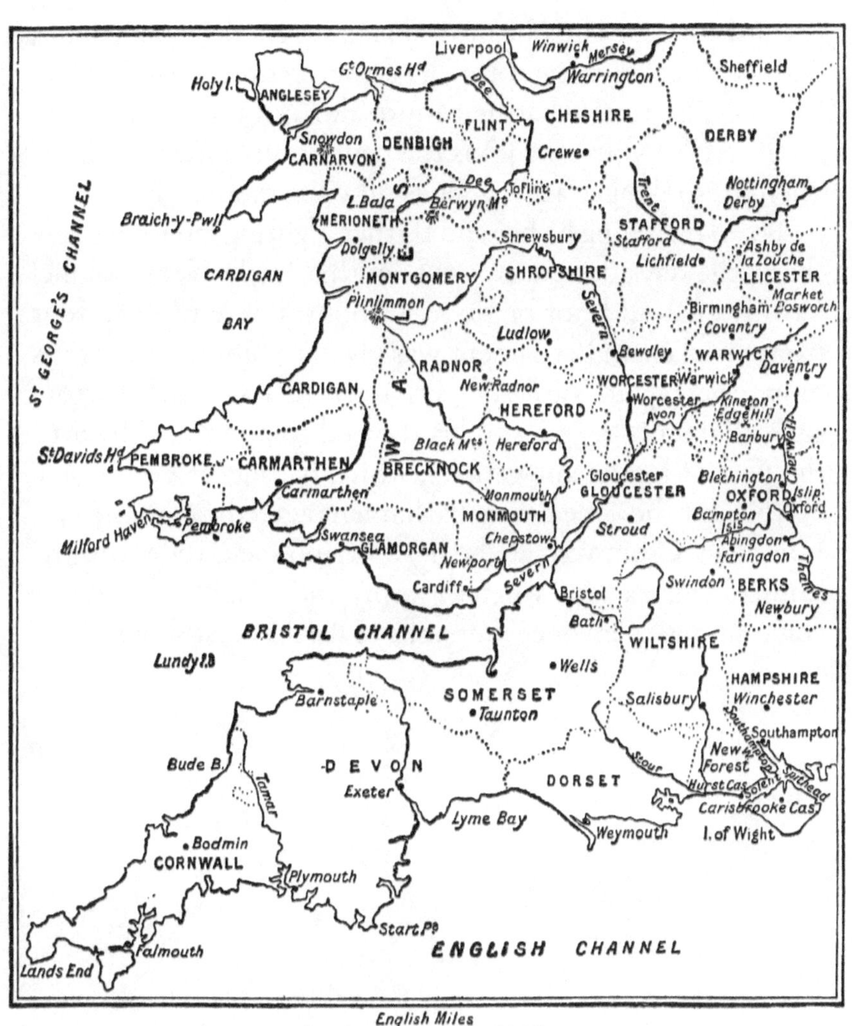

ST. GEORGE'S CHANNEL
Liverpool
Winwick
Mersey
Warrington
Sheffield
Holy I.
ANGLESEY
Gt Ormes Hd
CHESHIRE
DERBY
Snowdon
DENBIGH
FLINT
Crewe
CARNARVON
Nottingham
Derby
Braich-y-Pwll
Dee
Flint
L. Bala
Berwyn Mts
Trent
MERIONETH
STAFFORD
Dolgelly
Shrewsbury
Stafford
Ashby de
la Zouche
CARDIGAN
MONTGOMERY
SHROPSHIRE
Lichfield
LEICESTER
Plinlimmon
Birmingham
Market
Bosworth
BAY
Coventry
Ludlow
Severn
Bewdley
WARWICK
Daventry
CARDIGAN
RADNOR
WORCESTER
Warwick
New Radnor
Worcester
Kineton
Edge Hill
HEREFORD
Avon
Banbury
St Davids Hd
PEMBROKE
CARMARTHEN
BRECKNOCK
Black Mts
Hereford
Gloucester
Blechington
OXFORD
Islip
Carmarthen
Monmouth
GLOUCESTER
Oxford
Bampton
Isis
MONMOUTH
Stroud
Pembroke
Swansea
Chepstow
Abingdon
Faringdon
Milford Haven
GLAMORGAN
Newport
Severn
Swindon
BERKS
Cardiff
Bristol
Newbury
BRISTOL CHANNEL
Bath
WILTSHIRE
Lundy I.
Wells
HAMPSHIRE
Barnstaple
SOMERSET
Salisbury
Winchester
Taunton
Southampton
Bude B.
DEVON
New
Forest
Tamar
Exeter
DORSET
Stour
Hurst Cas
Solent
Spithead
Lyme Bay
Weymouth
Carisbrooke Cas
Bodmin
I. of Wight
CORNWALL
Plymouth
Start Pt
ENGLISH CHANNEL
Falmouth
Lands End
Thames
Cherwell
English Miles
0   10   20   30   40   50   60
W A L E S

struggling hard to remodel his army, found Oliver readiest to his hand, and sent him.

Then, back from Salisbury he comes, and is soon scouring Oxfordshire. At Islip, he meets and scatters the King's horse. At Blechington, at Bampton, he is successful. At Farringdon, for once, he tries what he cannot do, and fails to take the castle. At Newbury, he joins the new Commander-in-Chief. Then, fresh danger arising, he is off once more to Ely.

So, in marching hither and thither, fighting, now here now there, the days passed. It was seen that in the field Colonel Cromwell could not be done without. Leave to be absent from his place in Parliament was given to him for forty days more, then again for forty days, until, at last, Fairfax wrote to Parliament, begging to be allowed to appoint Oliver to the post of lieutenant-general, which had never been filled. To this, for the time being, Parliament agreed. So on the 13th June 1645, Cromwell, at the head of 600 men, rode into the camp of Fairfax. And when the army knew that Ironsides was come among them once more, they raised a great shout of joy.

Chapter 12

THE KING'S LAST BATTLE

NORTHAMPTONSHIRE is the very middle of the Midlands. Nine counties border upon it. It is one of the best agricultural counties of England, there being hardly any waste land in it. "Northampton is an apple without core to be cut out or rind to be pared away," says an old writer.

There are no coal fields in Northampton, and in consequence few factories. The same old writer we have already mentioned says, "It is enough for Northamptonshire to sell their wool, whilst other countries make cloth thereof. I speak not this to praise Northamptonshire men for not using, but that Northamptonshire men may praise God for not needing, manufactures. However, the town of Northampton may be said to stand chiefly on other men's legs, where the most and cheapest (if not the best) boots are bought in England." That was written 300 years ago, but it is still true to-day. And not only Northampton, but Kettering, Wellingborough, Rushden, Daventry, and indeed nearly every town and village along the eastern border and in the middle of the county may be said still to stand on other men's legs, for it is the great centre of the English boot trade. There boots are made for our soldiers, and, besides supplying all the great markets of England, many are exported to other countries, especially to our own colonies. Indeed, Northampton is one of the greatest boot-making centres of the world.

Northamptonshire is a tableland surrounded by low plains, and forms the central watershed of England. There rise the Nen, the Welland, and the Great Ouse, all flowing by different ways to Oliver's own fen-land, and falling at last into

Halifax
Wakefield
Huddersfield
Y O R K
Hull
Aire
Don
Trent
Gt Grimsby
Humber
Spurn Hd.
NORTH
SEA
Mablethorpe
The Peak
Sheffield
Gainsborough
Buxton
Rother
Chesterfield
Lincoln
Horncastle
Winceby
LINCOLN
Leek
DERBY
NOTTINGHAM
Southwell
Dove
Nottingham
Boston
Boston Deeps
Derby
Trent
Grantham
Witham
The Wash
Foulness
Fakenham
STAFFORD
Welland
The Fens
Lynn
G. Ouse
NORFOLK
Norwich
Yarmouth
Lichfield
Ashby de la Zouche
LEICESTER
RUTLAND
Oakham
Stamford
Nen
Swaffham
Watton
Lowestoft
Birmingham
Market Bosworth
Leicester
ISLE
OF
ELY
Attleborough
Waveney
Coventry
Naseby
Kettering
Stilton
Ely
Halesworth
NORTHAMPTON
Hinchinbrooke
St Ives
HUNTINGDON
Holmby Ho.
Huntingdon
CAMBRIDGE
Newmarket
SUFFOLK
WARWICK
Warwick
Daventry
Wellingborough
Rushden
St Neots
Cambridge
Cam
Avon
Northampton
Ipswich
Cropredy Br.
Bedford
Saffron Walden
Stour
Edge Hill
BEDFORD
The Naze
Banbury
Buntingford
Dunmow
Colchester
GLOUCESTER
WORCESTER
Blechington
BUCKINGHAM
HERTFORD
ESSEX
R Blackwater
OXFORD
Aylesbury
Hertford
Islip
Berkhampstead
St Albans
Chelmsford
Foulness I.
Bampton
Isis
Oxford
Brentwood
Abingdon
Faringdon
High Wycombe
Southend
Wooton Bassett
Uxbridge
MIDDLESEX
Barking
Mouth of the Thames
Henley
LONDON
Greenwich
Woolwich
Sheppey I.
N. Foreland
BERKSHIRE
Windsor
Brentford
Turnham Green
Blackheath
Reading
Egham
Staines
Hounslow
Rochester
Canterbury
Ramsgate
Newbury
Bagshot
Heath
WILTSHIRE
Woking
Caterham
K E N T
Tidworth
Basingstoke
SURREY
Dover
Andover
Guildford
Tonbridge
STRAIT OF DOVER
HAMPSHIRE
Horsham
Wadhurst
Cranbrook
Calais
Salisbury
Winchester
Midhurst
Uckfield
C. Gris Nez
DORSET
Southampton
S U S S E X
Battle
Hastings
Boulogne
New Forest
Avon
Portsmouth
Chichester
Hastings
FRANCE
Hurst Cas.
Southampton Water
Solent
Spithead
Selsea Bill
Brighton
Eastbourne
Beachy Head
Carisbrooke Cas.
I. of Wight
Ventnor
E N G L I S H   C H A N N E L
English Miles
10 5 0   10   20   30   40   50

the Wash. The Cherwell and the Avon (Shakespeare's Avon) rise there too, the one flowing to the Severn, and the other to the Thames by Oxford.

As Northamptonshire lies high, all its rivers flow out of it in different directions. None rising elsewhere flow through it as in other counties. It is upon this high ridge of Northamptonshire, almost in the middle of England, that the village of Naseby stands. And here it was that, for the last time, Charles I. faced the rebel army.

The numbers on either side were nearly even. But the King's soldiers were old and tried men, while many of the Parliamentarians had never before been in battle. For it was the first time that the "New Model" army, as it was called, had fought. The King, despising these new soldiers, made no doubt of beating them. But Oliver wrote, "I could not—riding alone about my business—but smile out to God in praises in assurance of victory."

At ten o'clock on the summer's morning, June 14th, the fight began. "God and Queen Mary," shouted the Royalists. "God with us," replied the Parliamentarians.

The battle almost seemed like Marston Moor over again. Prince Rupert charged, scattering all before him. But he pursued too far, and returned too late. Cromwell, too, charged, but having scattered the foe, he turned again, and came to help Fairfax and the foot-soldiers.

For three hours the battle waged. The day went ill for the King. "One charge more, and recover the day," he cried, trying to rally his broken men.

But a Scottish lord laid his hand upon the King's bridle, and, uttering strange oaths, cried, "Will you go upon your death in an instant?" and so crying he turned the King's horse. And being turned the King fled, not resting till he reached Leicester, sixteen miles away. After him and his flying troops thundered Cromwell and his horsemen, and hideous slaughter marked their path for many a mile, "Even to the sight of Leicester whither the King fled."

At Leicester the poor King found no rest. To Ashby de la Zouche he fled, then on to Litchfield, to Bewdley in Worcestershire, and at last to Hereford, where he had some vain hope of being able to gather another army.

But although Naseby had not quite finished the war, the King's cause was lost. He was henceforth like a hunted bird or driven leaf, flying now here, now there. At last, after months of wandering, he passed one night out of Oxford in the dark. His beautiful long hair was cut short, and he was dressed like a serving-man. Thus unknown, he travelled northward, until, ten days later, he rode into the camp of the Scots army, which lay at Southwell in Nottinghamshire.

Charles was a prisoner. Yet he might still have recovered his throne had he been willing to sign the Covenant, and promise to make England Presbyterian as Scotland was. But this he would not do, so the Scots gave him back to the English Parliament. They washed their hands of him, as it were, and marched away to their own country, leaving the English to settle the quarrel as best they might. But across the border they lay watching like couching lions, ready to spring if matters went not to their liking.

Chapter 13.

THE KING TAKES A JOURNEY

THE New Model army had proved victorious. The Civil War was at an end, and the King a prisoner. But the country was all in confusion, and soon a fight of another kind began.

The Puritans had already split into two parties—Presbyterians and Independents. Now these two parties took another form, and a struggle between the army and the Parliament began. For the Parliament was nearly all Presbyterian, and most of the soldiers were Independents.

The war being over, the Parliament wished to disband the army. They offered the soldiers eight weeks' pay, although nearly sixty was due to them. The soldiers grumbled at that, grew mutinous, and would not go.

Cromwell was at this time much in Parliament. He had moved his household to London, and his wife and family were now living in Drury Lane. Later, they went to another house nearer Westminster. Oliver talked, and voted, and wrote letters, trying very hard to smooth matters between the King, the Parliament, and the army. It was a hard task, and one which even he could not manage.

The army meantime lay encamped upon the chalk downs around Saffron Walden. In the autumn the fields about them were purple with crocus, from which saffron is made, and from which the village takes its name. Now these beautiful fields are seen no more, for about a hundred years ago the manufacture was given up, and much of the saffron we use comes from Germany.

One day, while the quarrel between the Parliament and the army was going on, a soldier, called Cornet Joyce, mounted his horse, and with five hundred men behind him, set out for Holmby House in Northamptonshire, where the King was kept prisoner.

More than half of Northamptonshire is pasture land, where sheep and cattle are bred and fattened for market. That is what makes leather so plentiful there, and is the cause of the boot factories being set up. Althorp, near which Holmby House stands, is specially noted for its "shorthorns."

As Cornet Joyce and his men rode along this sunny June weather, they would pass many a meadow where sheep and cattle grazed, many a copse where oak, and elm, and beech waved green in the summer sunshine. They passed through the town of Northampton, where, as the saying goes, "You know when you are within a mile of the town by the noise of the cobblers' lapstones." At length they came to Holmby.

At ten o'clock at night, Joyce knocked at the door, and demanded to see the King. Charles had gone to bed. But in spite of that Joyce insisted on seeing him. With his hat in one hand, and a cocked pistol in the other, he marched into the King's bedroom. "May it please your Majesty, I am sorry to disturb you out of your sleep," he said.

"No matter, if you mean me no harm," replied the King.

Then, politely and gently, Joyce told Charles that he must come with him. At first, however, the King refused to go. But after some talk he consented, and, as it was now late, he promised to be ready at six next morning. With this promise, Joyce left him.

True to his word, the King was ready at six next morning. When he came out to the steps of the house, he found Joyce and his men awaiting him, booted and spurred.

"I pray you, Mr. Joyce," said the King, "deal openly with me. Show me what commission you have "—meaning, show me a letter, so that I may know by whose orders you come to take me.

"Here is my commission," said Joyce.

"Where?" asked the King.

"Here," said Joyce again.

But the King could not understand. He looked about him. Still he saw no letter. "Where?" he asked once more.

"Behind me," said Joyce, pointing to his men, who sat there waiting, stern and quiet, in shining armour. "I hope that will satisfy your Majesty," he added.

The King now understood and smiled. "It is as fair a commission, and as well written as I have ever seen a commission in my life," he said. "A company of as handsome, proper gentlemen as I have seen a great while. But what if I refuse to go with you? I hope you will not force me. I am your King. You ought not to lay violent hands upon your King."

"We will do you no hurt, your Majesty," said Joyce. "Nay, we will not force you to go with us."

"How far do you mean to ride to-day? "said Charles, after a pause.

"As far as your Majesty conveniently can." Charles smiled. "I can ride as far as you or any man," he said. Then they set out.

That night, the King reached Hinchingbrooke House. It no longer belonged to Oliver's uncle, for he had spent so much money that he had been obliged to sell his grand house, and go to live in one much smaller. But did Charles, I wonder, remember that forty years before he had stayed in this same beautiful house, to which he now came a prisoner, as an honoured guest? And did he remember how he had fought with a little boy called Oliver?

Chapter 14

THE KING TAKES ANOTHER JOURNEY

WHEN the news of what Cornet Joyce had done was brought to London, Cromwell "lifted up his hands in Parliament and called God, angels and men to witness that he knew nothing of Joyce's going for the King."

But possession of the King, poor prisoner though he was, meant power, and now the army became more determined than before to resist the Parliament. So strong were the soldiers, indeed, that they demanded that eleven Presbyterian members who were their greatest enemies should be expelled from the House. And the eleven members ran away to hide themselves. The army, it would seem, was acting in a way not unlike the King, when he had tried to seize the famous five members.

The struggle between Parliament and army still went on. The army moved from place to place—to St. Albans, to Berkhampstead, to Uxbridge, to High Wycombe—and with them went the King, always treated with courtesy and lodged in some great house near.

The quarrels grew worse. All London sided with Parliament. But the army was so strong that the Commons were like to give way to them. Then one day a mob of young men rushed into the House. With clamour and shouting, they forced both Lords and Commons to vote as they wished. It was a scene of riot and disorder, such as never before had been known in Parliament.

This made matters no better, and at last, the Speakers of both Houses, some Lords, and many Commons, rode out to

KING CHARLES AND CORNET JOYCE.

join the army. "Lords and Commons and a Free Parliament!" shouted the soldiers as they came.

A few days later, Cromwell and Fairfax marched to London at the head of twenty thousand men, bringing the Speakers and members with them. Grim, stern men, heroes of Marston and Naseby, they came from Putney to Hyde Park, and on through the streets, until the doors of Westminster closed upon the returning members.

The struggle still went on. Oliver was always in Parliament at this time. "I feared to miss the House a day, where it is very necessary for me to be," he writes. Then one day came astonishing news. The King had escaped, and had fled to Carisbrooke Castle, in the Isle of Wight.

The Isle of Wight is a beautiful little island which lies to the south of England, off the coast of Hampshire. Once, long before the beginning of history, it formed part of the mainland. But the constant washing of the waves has worn a channel through the clay soil of the Plain of Southampton, as that part of Hampshire which borders on the sea is called, cutting Wight off from the mainland, and forming it into an island. People can guess this, because the north of the island is of clay soil like the Plain of Southampton, and the south is of chalky downs like those which surround the plain.

The Isle of Wight is four-cornered, not unlike a kite in shape. It lies with one of its corners pointing inland, forming a three-cornered strait. On the west this strait is called the Solent. On the east it is called Spithead. From the middle of this strait Southampton Water runs northward, the whole being something like a Y turned upside down, and forming a fine natural harbour. Except for a few sandbanks, which are known and marked, the water is everywhere deep. It gives splendid anchorage for men-of-war, the largest of which can sail there. So behind this sheltering island has grown up the greatest dockyard in the world—Portsmouth.

Portsmouth is really five towns in one—Portsmouth, Portsea, Landport, Southsea, and Gosport. It is not a commercial port like Southampton, which lies on Southampton Water. For it has neither coal fields nor iron fields to bring commerce there. But, on the other hand, the harbour is so large that the whole British Navy can lie there at once. It lies opposite the great French arsenal of Cherbourg, and is easily reached from London, all of which would make it useful in time of war. So it has become the great naval arsenal of the country.

Here in the huge dockyards, men-of-war are built and repaired. Here are stored vast quantities of tea, coffee, cocoa, tobacco, flour, oatmeal, guns, shot, shell, coal, anchors, boats, and everything, in fact, which is needed to fit vessels for sea. And to keep it all safe there are land batteries, sea batteries, forts, and barracks full of soldiers, all around. To guard the passage into Spithead, forts have even been built out in the sea, so that there is a chain of them between the mainland and the Isle of Wight.

Ever since the time of Henry VIII. Portsmouth has been famous. It was here, during his reign, while the French and English were fighting off Spithead, that the words from which our national anthem is made were first used. During the night the English watchword was "God save the King," and the reply, "Long to reign over us."

Many things have happened at Portsmouth, but perhaps the saddest was the loss of the *Royal George*. It went down in 1782, right in the road-stead. For many a year after, the hulk lay there, a great danger to shipping. No one knew how to get it up, but at last, in 1844, it was blown up.

It was from Spithead that Nelson sailed so often to victory, and off the dockyard of Portsmouth lies his ship the *Victory*.

Every year, on the anniversary of Trafalgar, it is decorated with laurels.

It is at Spithead that all the great naval reviews take place, such as those at Queen Victoria's jubilee and diamond jubilee. At the last, there was a display of five rows of ships, extending for three miles.

So you see what an important place Portsmouth is. If Charles could have kept it, it would have been of great service to him. But at the very beginning of the Civil War, the fleet had declared for the Parliament, and Portsmouth had fallen into their hands. The Isle of Wight too, after some fighting, had yielded to them, and Carisbrooke was now under a Parliamentarian governor. Yet, knowing this, Charles fled there. He hoped, perhaps, to make friends with the governor, who would let him escape to France. For it is easy to reach France from the Isle of Wight. But Charles was disappointed. He soon found that he was now more strictly kept a prisoner than he had ever been by the army.

Chapter 15

THE SECOND CIVIL WAR

IN the early spring of 1648, Oliver fell ill. For a time there was great trouble and sorrow in his home, for it was thought that he would die. But at last he began to get better. "It hath pleased God to raise me out of a dangerous sickness," he writes. "I received in myself the sentence of death that I might learn to trust in Him that raiseth from the dead."

And now he had need of all his strength and energy again. Now it was time for the army and the Parliament to forget their quarrels and work together. For months the country had been full of unrest. The Royalists, it is true, had been beaten, the King was a prisoner. But there were still many in the land who were ready to fight for him. At last they broke out, and what is called the Second Civil War began.

In London a captain of train-bands was attacked by a mob of young men crying, "King Charles, King Charles." The men of Kent marched to Blackheath, in arms. But Fairfax routed them and drove them back to Rochester. They took Canterbury, however, and tried to take Dover. In Essex too there was fighting. But there again Fairfax beat them, and drove them into Colchester, which he began to besiege. A Scots army, it was said, was marching once more over the Border, this time to fight, not for the Parliament, but for the King. So a Parliamentarian officer, named Lambert, was sent to meet them. The Welsh too had risen, under some revolted Parliamentarians, and against them marched Cromwell. On all sides the fires of war had burst forth again.

With rapid marches Cromwell rode across England. With

him were his own men—his Ironsides, and a company of men under Colonel Pride. Of Colonel Pride you will hear again.

Wales is a country full of mountains. Its people are kindly and friendly, easily pleased, easily made angry, "His Welsh blood is up" being a proverb. They are not English, these people, but are the descendants of the old Britons who, when the English came from over the sea, were driven from their homes by them. They were driven back, step by step, across the island, until they found a refuge among the mountains of the west. There, through hundreds of years, they lived safe from the conquering English, for these heathen foes dared not follow the old Britons into the lonely, barren, mountain passes.

There are four ranges of mountains in Wales— the Snowdon Mountains, the Berwyn Mountains, the Plinlimmon Mountains, and the Black Mountains. The little country is so full of them that there seems to be hardly room for anything else. Only along the valleys of the rivers there is a little cultivated land, where corn grows. But on the hillsides, hundreds and thousands of sheep graze, and, in Cardiganshire and Montgomeryshire, ponies too. The valleys are dotted with little agricultural towns, and the hillsides with sheep-farms, but in places one may wander for miles without seeing a human being, without hearing a sound except the bleat of sheep, the rush and tumble of a brook or the cry of wild birds.

Unlike the hill country of Scotland and the north of England, Wales has no lakes, or at least only one called Bala, in Merionethshire. But it has many mountain tarns and rushing streams, none of them, however, because of the nature of the land, being of much use for commerce. But, although the country is poor in agriculture, and in the north poor in commerce too, it is rich in beautiful scenery. Every year many visitors flock to Wales, drawn there by the loveliness of hill and valley. So wealth is brought in another way to the people.

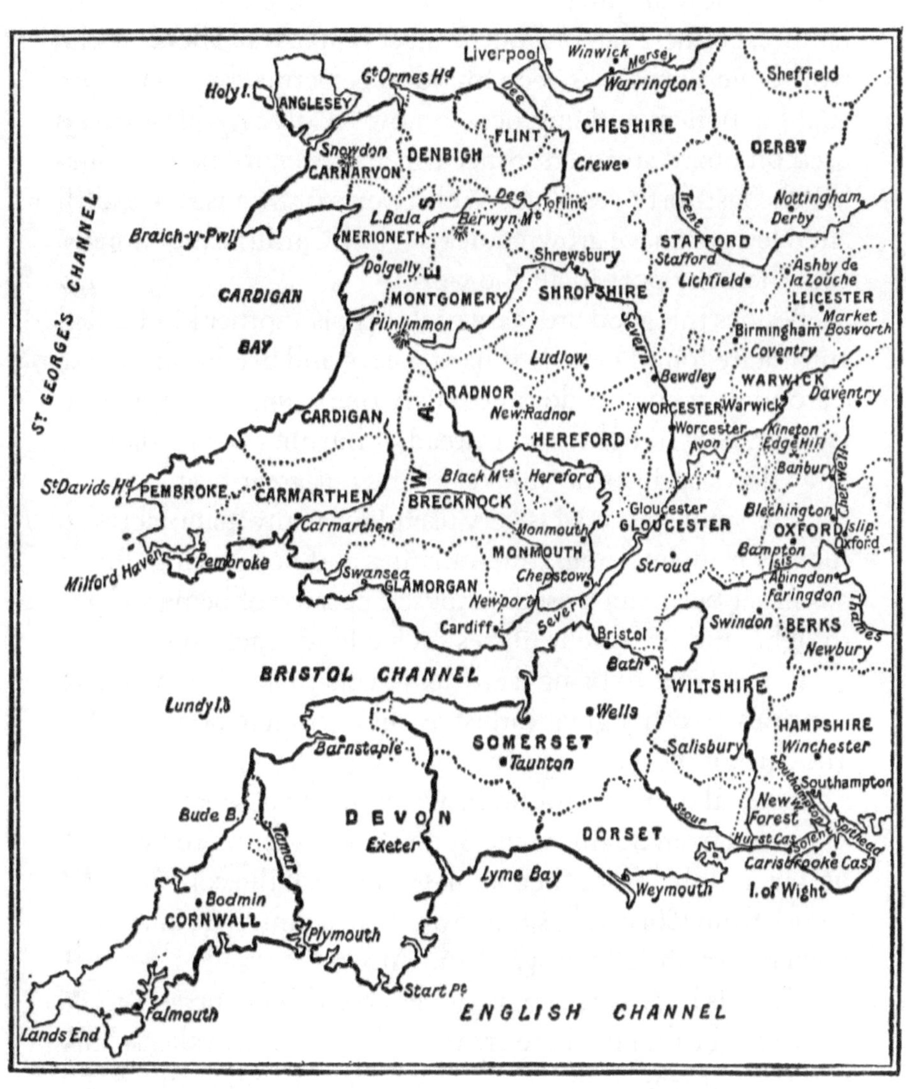

St George's Channel
Holy I.
ANGLESEY
Gt Ormes Hd
Liverpool
Winwick
Mersey
Warrington
Sheffield
CHESHIRE
FLINT
DERBY
Snowdon
DENBIGH
Crewe
CARNARVON
Braich-y-Pwll
L.Bala
Dee
To Flint
Berwyn Mts
Nottingham
Derby
MERIONETH
Trent
STAFFORD
Stafford
Shrewsbury
Dolgelly
Ashby de la Zouche
CARDIGAN
MONTGOMERY
SHROPSHIRE
Lichfield
LEICESTER
Plinlimmon
Market Bosworth
BAY
Birmingham
Coventry
Ludlow
Severn
WARWICK
Bewdley
Daventry
RADNOR
Warwick
CARDIGAN
New Radnor
WORCESTER
WALES
HEREFORD
Worcester
Kineton
Avon
Edge Hill
St Davids Hd
PEMBROKE
Black Mts
Hereford
Banbury
Cherwell
CARMARTHEN
BRECKNOCK
Blechington
Carmarthen
Gloucester
OXFORD
Islip
Monmouth
GLOUCESTER
Oxford
MONMOUTH
Bampton
Isis
Milford Haven
Pembroke
Swansea
Chepstow
Stroud
Abingdon
GLAMORGAN
Faringdon
Newport
Severn
Thames
Cardiff
Swindon
BERKS
Bristol
Newbury
BRISTOL CHANNEL
Bath
WILTSHIRE
Lundy I.
Wells
HAMPSHIRE
Barnstaple
SOMERSET
Salisbury
Winchester
Taunton
Southampton
Southampton
Bude B.
Tamar
DEVON
New Forest
Spithead
Exeter
DORSET
Hurst Cas.
Solent
Bodmin
Lyme Bay
Carisbrooke Cas.
CORNWALL
Plymouth
Weymouth
I. of Wight
Start Pt
ENGLISH CHANNEL
Lands End
Falmouth

In the south of the country, the part through which Cromwell was now marching, everything is different. Here there is no loneliness or quiet. It is a busy stir of mining and manufacture. For here lies one of the most famous coal fields of the world. Welsh coal has been found to be better than any other coal for boilers and engines, so now hardly anything else is used on board steamers. Since this has been found out, during the last forty years, the Welsh ports of Swansea, Cardiff, and Newport have grown quickly. Now Cardiff exports more coal than any port in all the world.

Besides this good ordinary coal there is another kind called anthracite found here. It is hard, heavy and bright, more like a stone than coal. It does not dirty one's fingers to touch it. It is not easy to light, and instead of burning with a flame it only glows and has no smoke, giving out great heat.

This smokeless coal is very useful for many manufactures, such as iron-smelting, lime-burning and hop-drying. But it has never been much used in houses, because of being so hard to light, and because it makes such a loud crackling.

It is cheaper to bring factories to coal than to carry coal to factories, so other great industries have risen in South Wales. The chief of these are copper- and iron-smelting. And although a good deal of iron is found in Wales, much of what is used is imported from Spain, as the Spanish ore is found to be much better, and therefore cheaper in the end. Of the copper, some comes from Cornwall, some from South America, and some is even brought all the way from Australia.

Wales is but a small country, yet no greater contrasts could anywhere be found. There are rugged hills, sunny valleys, busy ports, quiet seaside villages, noisy smoky manufacturing and mining towns, all within its borders. There, among the mountains, the air and sky are clear and blue; in the coal district the air is thick with smoke, and the sky lurid with flames.

Chapter 16

THE TAKING OF PEMBROKE CASTLE

NOW, in May 1648 all Wales, both north and south, was in a ferment. Everywhere, men might be seen wearing blue and white ribbons in their caps, with the words, "We want to see our King," written upon them. As Cromwell marched upon them, the people fled from their houses to the mountains. They took their goods with them, and destroyed what they could not carry away. "If you would give forty shillings for a horse-shoe, or a place to make it, it is not to be had," says one writer, so desolate was the land.

By Monmouth, Chepstow, Swansea and Carmarthen, Cromwell marched, fighting as he went, until he reached the castle of Pembroke.

On a high ridge thrust out into the sea, which washes it on two sides, Pembroke Castle stands, looking out upon Milford Haven, one of the finest natural harbours in the world. Curving into many creeks and bays it stretches ten miles inland. Here the largest ships may pass with ease, and sheltered by the surrounding hills the whole British fleet might safely anchor.

Many times in English history Milford Haven has played a part. It was from here that Henry II. sailed forth to the conquest of Ireland. It was here that Henry of Richmond landed on his way to win the crown of England, on Bosworth field. Here, now, are Royal dockyards, where war vessels of all sizes are built. But although Milford Haven is such a fine harbour it does not grow great as a trading port, for it lies too much out of the way of the chief highways of commerce.

Yet it is certain that Milford Haven will one day come to

greater importance, for it is about two hundred miles nearer America than either Liverpool or Southampton, and by starting from here the most dangerous part of the voyage would be missed. Then its splendid harbour, which has neither shoals nor bar, will be valued as it ought to be.

Though ruined now, Pembroke Castle, when Oliver came to besiege it, was very strong, having both an outer and inner wall. Cromwell had no great cannon fit to shatter these walls. So for six weeks his army lay before the castle waiting for hunger to do its work.

Outside the walls, in Cromwell's camp, things were bad enough. The country was poor and deserted, and there was little to be had for the men to eat but bread, and nothing to drink but water. They had only a few small cannon, which Oliver says he "scraped up." Yet with them he succeeded, at last, in doing some damage to the massive walls.

Within the castle things were much worse. The men were starving. They hated their leader, and were ready to mutiny and kill him. At last the weary, hungry men could hold out no longer, and in the beginning of July they yielded to Cromwell.

The three chief Royalists were condemned to death. But Cromwell afterwards decided that only one should die. It was settled by lot who should live, the lots being drawn by a child. Upon two of the papers was written "Life given by God." Upon the third was nothing. He to whom the third lot fell, died.

As soon as Pembroke Castle was taken, Cromwell marched back into England, to help Lambert against the Scots. His men were ragged and almost barefoot. They had had but little to eat while in Wales. They had not been paid for months. But they were tough and strong-hearted, and as unconquerable as ever. And now, if they had only known it, the fate of the whole kingdom was in their hands. For the Scots and English

Royalists were twenty-one thousand strong, and if they once reached London there was little doubt that the King would be King again.

But Cromwell knew this, and so he pushed on in haste to prevent them marching to London. At Leicester, his barefoot army was supplied with boots sent from Northampton, and with stockings from Coventry. Then he joined Lambert at Knaresborough, in Yorkshire. Together their forces numbered only eight thousand men, horse and foot.

And with this small force Cromwell had to keep watch across two counties. For whether the Royalist would march to London through Lancashire or through Yorkshire, he did not know. The Royalists, however, decided to go through Lancashire, for they hoped by that way to join other Royalists, who had risen in North Wales and in Hereford. As soon as Cromwell was sure of the way that they would go, he came by quick marches to Skipton and Gisburne, and down the valley of the Ribble to Stonyhurst, to stop the path.

Chapter 17.

ABOUT OLIVER'S NEXT
BATTLE-FIELD

LANCASHIRE, the county into which Cromwell now marched, is one of the most important in England. It was one, too, which had suffered very much from the war. There was hardly a town of any size which had not been besieged, hardly a village where there had not been a skirmish. It was the nature of the country itself which made this to be so. In the north, it is agricultural and pastoral. There, lived gentlemen and Cavaliers who sided with the King. In the south, it is full of busy manufacturing towns, whose citizens and traders sided with the Parliament. So north and south fought.

The reason for this division is easily found. The north is chiefly hill and moor, only suitable for grazing and tilling. But in the south lies a great coal field. And where there is coal, there factories come.

This coal field is really the same as the Yorkshire coal field. But thousands and thousands of years ago by some great earth shaking, the Pennine range was thrown up, breaking it in two. Like the Welsh coal field, the Lancashire has a special kind of coal, called cannel, found chiefly round Wigan. It is a dull greyish black or brown, but it is so hard that it can be cut and polished like jet. It lights easily and burns brightly. That is how it came to have its name, which really means *candle*. Long ago, the Lancashire peasants used to like this coal to burn in the long winter evenings, for its flame was so bright they needed no candles. Now it is chiefly used for making gas, and a great deal of it is exported to Ireland.

Besides coal, Lancashire has iron ore. This is chiefly found

Berwick
SCOTLAND
Tweed
Cheviot Hills
Alnwick
NORTHUMBERLAND
Nith
NORTH
Newcastle
Tyne
SEA
Solway firth
Carlisle
Pennine
Durham
CUMBERLAND
Wear
DURHAM
WESTMORLAND
Tees
Cleveland
Swale
Moors
Northallerton
Furness
Kirkby
Lonsdale
Chain
Y O R K
Wolds
Barrow
IRISH
Knaresborough
York
Stamford Br.
SEA
Skipton
Marston Moor
Hull
Gisburne
Ouse
Stonyhurst
Ribble
Towton
Preston Moor
Aire
Hull
Preston
Halifax
Humber
LANCASHIRE
Barnsley
Trent
Wigan
Manchester
Liverpool
Winwick
Sheffield
Gainsborough
Dee
Mersey
Warrington
LINCOLN
CHESHIRE
DERBY
NOTTINGHAM
Horncastle
Winceby
DENBIGH FLINT
English Miles
0   10   20   30   40   50   60

in Furness, lying in that part of the county to the north, which really, so far as geography goes, ought to belong to Cumberland. It is only within the last sixty years that these mines have been discovered and worked. So Barrow is a good example of how quickly the discovery of coal or iron will turn quiet country into busy, smoky town. Sixty years ago there were only a few cottages in the village of Barrow, with scarcely three hundred people living in them. To-day Barrow is a large town with nearly sixty thousand inhabitants. Smelting furnaces belch forth fire, steel works, brick works, rope works, shipbuilding yards, and miles of dock cover the ground where, but a few years ago, grass and corn waved; and great ships ride at anchor where there was then but a single fishing smack.

But it is for its cotton manufactures that Lancashire is most famous. Just as Yorkshire, because of its moors and wolds, upon which so many sheep graze, has become the centre of woollen factories, so Lancashire, for other reasons, has become the centre of cotton factories.

Cotton is best spun in a somewhat damp climate, as the thread will then bear a greater strain upon it. And, low though they are, the Pennines catch the rain-laden winds which blow from the Atlantic. This makes the climate of Lancashire moister than that of Yorkshire. Before the power of steam was discovered, mills could only be built where there was water-power. Many streams fed by the rains flow from the slopes of the Pennines, and there cotton factories were built. It is from America that most of the raw cotton comes, and Liverpool, looking as it does towards America, is the port by which it can most easily be brought into the country, so that is another reason for building cotton factories on the west, within easy reach of Liverpool, which lies upon the Mersey.

Except the Thames, no river in the world is so busy as the Mersey. Except London, no town in the kingdom has so much trade as Liverpool. And it has a great advantage over London in lying near a coal field. Its docks are perhaps the finest in the world, and it has forty miles of quay. Here all kinds of merchandise may be seen; grain, cotton, and cattle from America; butter and eggs and all kinds of dairy produce from Ireland; besides tobacco and wood and all sorts of things from every part of the world.

The very centre of this centre of the cotton trade is Manchester. It is a busy, crowded city, and through its streets flow several streams, inky with dye from works beyond the town. Although not many cotton goods are actually made in Manchester, it is here where the spinners and weavers, printers and bleachers, from the busy towns and villages around, meet to buy and sell. Four hundred years ago Manchester was already famous for its cotton trade, and three hundred years ago it was said, "Other things being made in Manchester are so small in themselves, and various in their kinds, they will fill the shop of a haberdasher of smallwares. Being, therefore, too many for me to reckon up and remember, it will be the safest way to wrap them all together in some Manchester ticking, and to fasten them with the pins (to prevent their falling out and scattering), to tie them with the tape, and also (because sure bind sure find) to bind them about with points and laces, all made in the same place."

Chapter 18

A THREE DAYS' BATTLE

IT was through this busy Lancashire, of which we have been reading in the last chapter, that Cromwell came marching to meet the Scots. The Scots leader, the Duke of Hamilton, was a bad general. His officers quarrelled among themselves and with the English Royalists, and he was not strong enough to make them agree and do as he commanded. Each wanted to go his own way, yet there was no great man among them who could force them to act together. Indeed, he would have been a clever man who could have made Scots Presbyterians and English Episcopalians do that.

Hamilton's line of march was so long and straggling, that his army was really divided into three parts. Most of the horse was at Wigan; Hamilton himself at Preston, fifteen miles behind, and a third party at Kirby Lonsdale, in Westmorland, thirty miles still farther off, when Cromwell attacked them.

It was upon the English Royalists under Langdale, and a few Scottish horse under Hamilton, that the first shock of battle fell. For four hours they fought gallantly in the hedge-ringed fields of Preston Moor. But from hedge to hedge they were beaten back, till at last, with ranks broken and disordered, they fled towards Preston pursued by the Ironsides. Through the streets they fled, and over the bridge which crossed the Ribble, then scattering, some fled northward to carry the news of disaster to the Scottish foot; some southward to Wigan; some they knew not where. Of the army which had fought that day on Preston Moor, few indeed remained, for a thousand lay dead upon the field, and four thousand more were prisoners—"nothing hindering the ruin of that part of the enemy's army but the night," wrote Cromwell. "Where Langdale and his broken forces are I know not; but they are exceedingly shattered."

In the Scottish camp there was gloom and despair, yet the leaders were no more united than before. Some wanted to make a stand and fight where they were. Others wished to march away in the darkness and try to join the horse at Wigan. This they decided to do. They had no horses to carry their baggage and ammunition. All must be left behind. So each man filled his powder-flask, and the rest was left to fall later into the hands of Cromwell. Then, without sound of drum or pipe, in the rain and silence of the night, the already weary, hungry men began their march southward. So quietly did they go, so weary were the pursuing Ironsides, that they were already three miles on the way before Cromwell found out that they had gone. Then he started in pursuit.

While the Scottish foot were thus marching southward in the rain and dark, the horse from Wigan marched northward to meet them. They went, however, by different roads, and so missed each other. But Middleton, the leader of the horse, finding out his mistake, turned back again, and, coming between the foot soldiers and Cromwell's pursuing army, beat him back again and again.

So at last, the weary soldiers reached Wigan. They were faint with hunger, wet to the skin and covered with mud, for it had poured with rain all day and the roads were like marshes. Cromwell and his men were close behind and encamped outside the town, being "very dirty and weary, and having marched twelve miles of such ground as I never rode in all my life," says Cromwell.

But there was no rest for the weary Scots with the terrible Ironsides pursuing. Having plundered Wigan, Royalist town although it was, for food and clothes, they marched on again, hoping to reach Warrington and put the Mersey between themselves and their foes.

The heavy rainclouds now blew over, and a watery moon shone out. It shone upon those who wearily fled, and upon those who, almost as weary, pursued. Next morning at Winwick, a few miles from Warrington, Cromwell came up with the Scots. Again there was a desperate fight. Again the Royalists were defeated. Leaving behind them a thousand dead and two thousand prisoners, they continued the spiritless march. After them came the Ironsides; but the chase was nearly over. At Warrington, four thousand more surrendered to Cromwell, Hamilton and a few thousand horse only escaping. "They (the Scots) are so tired and in such confusion," writes Cromwell, "that if my horse could but trot after them, I could take them all. But we are so weary, we can scarce be able to do more than walk after them. They are the miserablest party that ever was. I durst engage myself, with five hundred fresh horse, and five hundred nimble foot, to destroy them all. My horse are miserably beaten out; and I have ten thousand prisoners."

The three days' fight named from Preston was over. "A wonderful great mercy and success," the Parliament called it. The great Royalist army of the North was utterly crushed by a force scarcely one-third its size. The fleeing remnants, one way or another, fell into the hands of Cromwell. And so the second Civil War ended, having lasted only a few months. Of the ten thousand prisoners, some were allowed to go free, after promising never again to take up arms against the Parliament. Others were sent as slaves to the plantations of Virginia and the West Indies.

Chapter 19

OLIVER'S FIRST VISIT
TO SCOTLAND

THE second Civil War was really over. But Oliver always liked to do what he had in hand thoroughly. So, "to make an end of the business of Scotland," he marched northward. Back, across the Pennines, into Yorkshire he went once more. Then northward, now riding through wild moor-land, now tramping down the long, wide street of Northallerton, passing not far from the famous battle-field of the Standard; across the Tees and Wear, by the bare plains of Durham, now smoky with collieries, to Durham itself with its grand cathedral and frowning castle perched above the town; by Alnwick with its castle, so often the scene of strife between Englishman and Scot, nearer and nearer to the border, until he came to Berwick-on-Tweed.

Once Berwick was a great seaport. Now it is of little note except for its salmon fisheries. Lying as it does on the border, it has been fought and struggled for more than any other town. It had belonged now to one country, now to the other, until at length it was made into a county by itself, and still remains so.

But Cromwell did not now want to fight with the Scots. He knew that many of them were still on the side of the Parliament. It was only the "Engagers," as those who had followed Hamilton were called, who were on the King's side. So, from Alnwick, Oliver wrote letters to the leaders of the Scottish Parliament, telling them that he came in peace. And, welcomed as a friend, the great soldier rode towards Edinburgh.

It was an October day on which he first saw the grey old

CROMWELL IN EDINBURGH.

town sitting "Queen of the unconquered North" high upon her hills. Edinburgh is a city set upon hills and guarded by hills. There is Arthur's Seat couched like a sleeping lion, from which once the great British King, Arthur, looked down upon his fighting legions. There is the Calton with its monuments, and last, the rugged Castle rock, crowned with battlements, frowning down upon green gardens and upon the fairest street in all the kingdom.

Edinburgh takes its name from Edwin the Fair, King of Deira, who built a fort there in 629. But the Scots called it Dunedin—that is, the hill of Edwin. And it is often called the Maiden City, for there the daughters of the King used to live.

Edinburgh is the capital of, and, with its port of Leith, the second city in, Scotland. But although it has many advantages, although it is near a coal field and upon a waterway reaching far inland, and opposite the northern continental ports, it is not its trade which makes the city famous, but its beauty and its history.

The Castle, "crowned with battlements and towers," is full of memories. So too are the crowded narrow streets which lead from the Castle to the Palace of Holyrood—the palace in which kings and princes and fair queens have played their parts and passed away. Now Cromwell was feasted here "with a noble entertainment." In his heavy boots he tramped up and down the High Street and the Canongate, from his lodgings in the Earl of Moray's fine new house, to Holyrood and the Castle. He had many talks with the grave Scottish nobles and solemn divines, bending them to his will, as he bent all men.

Then, they having readily promised that none of the "Engagers" should ever again be allowed to have any power, Oliver marched home once more, well pleased with his work.

"I do think the affairs of Scotland are in a thriving posture as to the interest of honest men," he writes; "and Scotland is like to be a better neighbour to you now."

Meantime, while Cromwell was fighting and conquering in the north, the Parliament, freed from his overbearing will, were doing as they liked. Once more they tried to come to an agreement with the King. Once more letters and visits passed between them.

But the time when the King might have saved himself by giving in had gone. The army, looking on, grew more and more angry. They would have no more dealings with "Charles Stuart, that man of blood." They wished to punish him as the grand author of all their troubles. But the Parliament would not listen to the army, and went on trying to make an agreement with the King.

Then, early one winter's morning, an officer burst into the King's room, telling him to make ready to come with him. Again, as once before, the King asked to see his orders. But the officer refused to show any order. So, seeing nothing else for it, Charles said a sad farewell to the friends who were with him, and prepared to go.

Thus once again Charles was the prisoner of the army. This time he was taken to Hurst, a damp and dreary castle on the shores of Hampshire. It was lonely and desolate, being surrounded by water except where a narrow shingly path joined it to the land. The King had never given up hope of being at length able to escape. But now when he saw the thick walls of this dark and lonely castle, his heart sank within him.

Chapter 20

THE KING'S LAST JOURNEY

HAVING the King once more in their power, the army could now act. The morning after Charles had been carried to Hurst Castle, Fairfax and his men marched into London, taking possession of the city. Still, the Parliament was not to be frightened into doing what the army wanted them to do.

Then one morning at seven o'clock the heavy tramp of soldiers was heard around the House of Parliament. Armed men filled the courts, the lobby, and the stairs. At the door stood Colonel Pride with a paper in his hand. Upon this paper were the names of all those members who would not vote and act as the army wished. As soon as one of these appeared, he was turned back or seized and shut up in a room called the "Queen's Room." "By whose authority, by whose orders, is this done?" they asked.

"By the power of the sword," was the reply.

Next day Colonel Pride was again at his post. Member after member was turned back or taken prisoner, and by night-fall there were but fifty or sixty members left. Among them was General Cromwell, member for Cambridge, but newly returned from Scotland.

This is called "Pride's Purge," he having purged away all those who would not, according to his idea, do right. And the Parliament, being but now a remnant of a Parliament, was called "The Rump."

The army was master of the kingdom. It had become a tyrant, and its tyranny was as great as ever that of Charles had been. As the power of the army had grown, Cromwell's power had grown with it. But now it had become too strong even for him. It forced him to something which he had at first never meant to do. It forced him to bring the King to trial and to death.

But when once Cromwell became sure that the King must die, when he began to believe that in no other way would peace come to the country, nothing made him hesitate. So, from the lonely, dreary castle by the sea, the King was brought to Windsor. He came through the woodland of the New Forest to the royal town of Winchester, and on, by the chalky downs of Surrey, to Bagshot Heath, and at last to Windsor.

From there, a few days later, he was brought to London, to meet his stern judges. They accused him of being a tyrant, a traitor, a murderer, and a public enemy. They condemned him to die.

Charles had not been a good king. He had thought more of his own will than of the happiness of his people. But those were very hard times in which to rule. And now he met his death bravely and like a gentleman.

"There is but one stage more," said the bishop who was allowed to be with him on the scaffold. "It is very short, and in an instant will lead you a most long way, from earth to heaven, where you shall find great joy and comfort."

"I go," replied the King, "from a corruptible to an incorruptible crown, where can be no trouble, none at all."

An so he passed on his last journey.

Now that the poor King, who had caused so much sorrow and suffering, and who himself had had such a sad life, lay dead, his friends begged to be allowed to bury him. This they were permitted to do. It was winter time, and as they reverently carried the coffin, covered with black velvet, through the streets, the snow fell fast. And so, shrouded in white, the "White King," as he was often called, was laid to rest in St.

FUNERAL OF KING CHARLES.

George's Chapel at Windsor, "without any words or other ceremonies than the tears and sighs of the few beholders."

As soon as Charles was dead the Parliament declared that lords were useless and dangerous, and that they would have no more of them. They also said that kings were "unnecessary, burdensome, and dangerous to the liberty of the people." And that they would have no more of them, and that England should henceforth be a Commonwealth or Free State. Even before the King was beheaded, the Parliament had declared it to be against the law for any one to proclaim his son, Prince Charles, King. But the Scots, who had never meant that the King should be killed, were angry at what the English had done. They at once proclaimed Prince Charles King, and made ready to fight for him. The Irish did the same, and, besides this, there were many in England who were ready to join them. Soon the whole country was again in arms.

Chapter 21

ABOUT THE PLANTING OF ULSTER

DURING the whole time of the Civil War, Ireland had been in a state of confusion and rebellion such as would be hard to describe or understand. Englishmen and Irishmen, Protestants and Catholics, Royalists and Parliamentarians, all fought in a pell-mell of hatred. Yet now, most of them forgot their quarrels and joined against the murderers of the King.

Cromwell was full of wrath and hatred against the Irish. His anger made him cruel, and to understand, if not to excuse, this cruelty we must look back a little into the history of Ireland.

Although since the days of Henry II., the kings of England had called themselves Lords of Ireland too, it had often been little more than an empty title. The Irish were wild and rebellious, and except in the counties of Dublin, Meath, Kildare, and Louth, where Englishmen had settled, English rule was scarcely felt in Ireland. This part of Ireland was called the English Pale. Although many English lived there it was only as lords and masters. They never mixed with the Irish people.

Indeed they took care to dress differently and even cut their hair and shaved their faces in another fashion from the Irish, so that no one might mistake the one for the other.

The Irish hated these English tyrants, and there were often rebellions. In the days of the great Queen Elizabeth a rebellion under Hugh O'Neil, Earl of Tyrone, broke out. This rebellion lasted for several years, but at last, just before the great Queen died, O'Neil gave himself up. When King James came to the throne he forgave O'Neil and gave him back his title and lands. But a little later O'Neil was accused of treason and suddenly fled from the country with his friend and relation Rory O'Donnell, Earl of Tyrconnell, and about a hundred others. King James seized the land of these fugitives. In this way six counties of the province of Ulster—Donegal, Derry, Tyrone, Fermanagh, Cavan, and Armagh—came to the crown.

In these six counties there are about two million acres of land. But a million and a half was bog, mountain, and forest. Upon the other half million acres King James decided to settle English and Scottish Protestants. Already in Antrim and Down there were many Scottish folk who for hundreds of years had been quietly coming over from the barren highlands to make their homes among the green pastures of Ireland. So when the King's new settlers came nearly all the north of Catholic Ireland became Protestant. This is called the Plantation of Ulster. And it is from these old planters that many of the people of Ulster claim to be descended to-day.

In order to raise money to help the "planting of Ulster" James created a new title, that of baronet. This title, instead of being given to a man as a reward for some great service or brave deed, as titles usually were, might be bought. Any one who cared to pay £1095 could become a baronet.

As the first baronets were made at the planting of Ulster, all bear upon their coat of arms a bloody hand, which is the badge of Ulster. Of course people laughed at these upstart lords, but the new colonists were men accustomed to work and eager to work. They were men who already by brains and diligence had made money and position for themselves. They were not grand lords who only wished to win land that others might till it for them like the fine gentlemen of the English Pale. They were merchants, farmers, and traders. Among them there were weavers, mechanics, and labourers, so very quickly Ulster grew in wealth and prosperity.

The Irish looked upon these new comers with hatred. They were strangers who robbed them of the land of their fathers. They were also Protestants. The English of the Pale had at least been Catholics. In those far-off days people who could not think alike about worshipping God hated and dreaded each other, and each side, when it grew strong, tortured and persecuted the other. So the days of the Planting of Ulster were not altogether bright.

But when Strafford, the friend of King Charles, came to rule Ireland, matters grew worse. The Irish saw that he meant to take still more of their land and give it to the English and Scots, and they hated him. Strafford ruled like a tyrant. Yet he kept order and peace. Trade grew and the land prospered. But he built upon a volcano. The order was the order of force, the peace the peace of despair, and when at length Strafford was recalled and beheaded, Ireland was seething with hatred and wrath.

In the winter of 1641 this hatred broke into terrible rebellion. The Irish, under chiefs who had lost their lands by the Planting of Ulster, rose against the English and Scots settlers. Among the lonely farms and the little agricultural and industrial towns of Ulster, so newly sprung to life, there was terrible slaughter.

Men, women and children, alike, were slain, or cast adrift in the wintry weather, to die miserably of cold and hunger. Many dreadful deeds were done, for the Irish, who had suffered so much, had no pity. It was the memory of this terrible massacre which filled Cromwell's heart with bitterness and made him hard and cruel towards the Irish. For this he now determined to punish them and at the same time put down the rebellion.

So with his army he set out for Ireland. He was made Commander-in-Chief and Lord-Lieutenant of Ireland, and began his journey in great state. He drove in a fine coach drawn by six grey horses, and a bodyguard of gentlemen marched beside him. As he passed through the streets the people cheered and trumpets blew till it seemed as if Charing Cross shook to its foundations.

Chapter 22.

OLIVER GOES TO THE GREEN ISLAND

THE Lord-Lieutenant drove through England in state to Bristol. From there he went on through Wales to Pembroke Castle, from which but a few months before he and his hungry army had marched away ragged but victorious. There, in Milford Haven, ships lay ready to carry him over the Irish Sea. It was August, and the sea was rough, and "the Lord-Lieutenant was as sea-sick as ever I saw a man in my life." No doubt he was glad when the voyage was over, and he was safe at last within the blue waters of Dublin Bay.

Ireland is a very different country from Britain in many ways. It has no backbone of mountains, like England and Scotland, forming a *water-parting* range. Instead, the whole centre of the country is a plain, ringed round with mountains. As these mountains lie near the shore, the rivers rising there are very short and rapid, and of little use for commerce. There is one great river, however, called the Shannon. It is larger and longer than any river in the British Isles, and ships can sail up it for a greater distance. It rises in the north-west mountains, and crosses the great central plain, falling into the Atlantic on the south-west.

If Ireland were rich in coal fields like Britain this river would be of great use as a trading waterway. But, although there are a few coal fields in Ireland, they are not large enough to bring factories. They are not even large enough to supply all the coal that is needed for house use. So many people burn peat, which is cut from the bogs, of which there are many in the great central plain. Indeed one-seventh of the whole surface of Ireland is bog.

Ireland has good iron ore, and lead and copper too, but they are little worked. It is difficult to make it pay when coal has to be brought a great distance. As long as there were plenty of trees in Ireland, which could be cut down for wood, iron ore was worked. But now, although the climate and soil of Ireland are well suited for tree-growing, it is one of the worst wooded countries of Europe. On the whole, Ireland cannot be said to be either a manufacturing or a mining country.

The climate of Ireland is damper than that of Britain. Lying, as it does, between Britain and the Atlantic, its high mountains catch the heavy rain-clouds blowing from the west before they pass on. And although much of the land is very rich, being so damp, it is more suitable for pasture than for agriculture. So Ireland has become famous for its cattle, poultry, dairy produce, and horses.

Besides being divided into counties, as England and Scotland are, Ireland is divided into provinces. These are the five old kingdoms into which Ireland used to be divided long ago, each having a separate king. Their names were Ulster, Connaught, Munster, Leinster, and Meath. But Leinster and Meath are now one, so to-day there are four provinces.

Dublin, at which Cromwell now landed, is in the province of Leinster. Besides being the capital, Dublin is the finest town in Ireland. It lies upon the Liffey, which flows right through the town, and is crossed by many bridges. Although it is not a manufacturing town, it has two great industries, brewing and poplin making. The water of the streams here is good for making beer and for dyeing silk and wool. So Irish poplins and Guinness's stout are famous the world over.

Dublin is not naturally a good harbour, for the bay is full of sand-banks. So a harbour has been built at Kingstown, on the south shore of the bay, about six miles off. Through this port all the trade of Dublin passes. Lying opposite South

Lancashire, with its busy manufacturing towns, Kingstown has grown important.

From here, eggs, butter, poultry, and all kinds of farm produce are shipped across to feed the hungry workers. And to this port are brought tea, and coffee, and many other goods from foreign lands for the people of Ireland. For the valley of the Liffey, breaking through the ring of hills, makes Dublin a convenient place from which to carry goods inland, and to distribute them over the towns of the plain.

Dublin was in the hands of the Parliamentarians, and, when Cromwell landed, the people received him with great joy, cheering loudly as he and his men marched through the streets. But the capital was almost the only place except Londonderry left to the Parliamentarians in all Ireland, and Londonderry was besieged by Royalists.

Cromwell began at once to remodel the Irish army as he had remodeled the English. He found it full of bad men who drank, and swore and plundered. None of these things were allowed in Oliver's army, so he got rid of the bad men. He also proclaimed that soldiers must henceforth pay for what they took. Any who robbed the people should be punished. Then, having rested for a few days, he marched northward to Drogheda. He arrived there on the 3rd of September, which he always thought was his lucky day.

Chapter 23.

THE TAKING OF DROGHEDA

DROGHEDA means the bridge of the ford. It lies upon the river Boyne, and, like Dublin, it is built on both banks of the river. But, in the days of Cromwell, there was only one bridge over it, and all round were strong walls.

It lies near a farming district, and is the most important export town in that part of Ireland. From there butter and eggs are sent to England. It has linen manufactures too, for which many Irish towns are famous.

Now the Royalists made a brave defence, but Cromwell had heavy guns with which he battered the walls, until he made a breach. Then his soldiers rushed at the breach, hoping to storm the town. But so fiercely did the Royalists fight that they were thrown back. Again they rushed to the attack. Again they were thrown back.

Then Cromwell, seeing how his men were baffled again and again, put himself at their head. New courage came to the Ironsides, and shouting with joy, they followed their gallant leader. And as the sun was sinking, the town at last was won. Back and back the brave defenders were borne to the Mill Mount, the highest and strongest place in the town. Even here the Ironsides followed, and almost to a man the Royalists were slaughtered where they stood.

In his wars in England Cromwell had been stern and fierce. Now he was pitiless. No mercy was shown. "No quarter" was the cry. Over the bridge fled the Royalists pursued by the conquerors. There was no safety anywhere. A church in which some took refuge was set on fire, and the poor wretches within it died in the flames. The blaze of the burning church lit up the darkness, for night had now fallen, and as the bloodshed went on the shrieks of the dying mingled with the roar of flames, and the crash of falling stones.

So awful was the slaughter, that of three thousand men scarcely thirty escaped. Not only soldiers, but all the friars and priests within the town were "knocked on the head." Thus the siege of Drogheda ended in a fearful and pitiless butchery.

Cromwell himself, even in those rough, stern times, felt the need of some excuse. He gave the order for "no quarter," he said, in the heat and anger of battle. And such bitterness would serve, he thought, as an example to the rebels and prevent bloodshed in future, "Which are the satisfactory grounds to such actions, which otherwise cannot but work remorse and regret."

The slaughter of Drogheda struck terror, for a time at least, into the hearts of the Royalists. Trim, a little agricultural town farther up the Boyne, gave in without striking a blow. Dundalk, which like Drogheda is a trading seaport, followed.

Then Cromwell, leaving garrisons to guard his conquests, marched southward by Wicklow and Limerick, to Wexford, castles and towns yielding to him everywhere as he marched.

This Limerick is not the seaport on the west, the chief town of the county of Limerick, but a little village in Wexford.

Cromwell wanted to take Wexford because the bay was a natural harbour, easily reached from Milford Haven, where troops could be landed. From the south of the bay a tongue of land, ending in Rosslare Point, runs northward forming Wexford Harbour, and at Rosslare there is now a good harbour. Between Dublin Bay and Wexford there is no other good inlet. The county of Wexford, sloping towards the sea from the Arklow and Wicklow mountains, is very fertile. It has become famous for its butter and eggs and dairy produce, which are easily shipped off to other places through the port

NORTH CHANNEL
L. Swilly
Malin Hd.
Bloody Foreland
Rathlin I.
Moville
L. Foyle
Coleraine
Aranmore I.
Londonderry
LONDONDERRY
ANTRIM
Larne
DONEGAL
Lifford
Bann
Castle Dawson
Antrim
Belfast L.
Rossan Pt.
Donegal
TYRONE
ULSTER
L. Neagh
Belfast
Donegal Bay
Strangford L.
L. Erne
DOWN
Sligo B.
FERMANAGH
Armagh
Erris Hd.
Sligo
L. Erne
Monaghan
ARMAGH
Newry
Dundrum B.
Killala
SLIGO
MONAGHAN
Dundalk
L. Conn
LEITRIM
Cavan
CAVAN
Dundalk B.
Achill Hd.
MAYO
Carrick
on Shannon
LOUTH
Achill I.
Castlebar
ROSCOMMON
Drogheda
R. Boyne
IRISH
Clare I.
CONNAUGHT
LONGFORD
SEA
L. Mask
MEATH
Mannin B.
Tuam
Lune
Mullingar
Trim
Slyne Hd.
L. Corrib
L.
Ree
WEST MEATH
DUBLIN
Dublin B.
GALWAY
Suck
DUBLIN
Kingstown
Galway
Ballinsloe
Liffey
Galway Bay
Shannon
KINGS CO.
KILDARE
Wicklow Mts.
Aran I.
LEINSTER
Wicklow
Mal B.
CLARE
L.
Derg
QUEENS CO.
WICKLOW
Ennis
Carlow
Loop Hd.
Kilkenny
CARLOW
Limerick
R. Shannon
Limerick
TIPPERARY
KILKENNY
Barrow
LIMERICK
Cashel
WEXFORD
Tralee
MUNSTER
Fethard
New Ross
Wexford Harb.
Caher
Clonmel
Wexford
Rosslare Pt.
Rosslare Harb.
Blackwater
Waterford
WATERFORD
Carnsore Pt.
Dingle B.
KERRY
Youghal
Hook Hd.
CORK
Lee
Youghal B.
St. Davids Hd.
Cork
Bandon Bn.
Kinsale
Cork Har.
Old Head of Kinsale
ST. GEORGE'S CHANNEL
Mizen Hd.
Cape Clear
ATLANTIC OCEAN
English Miles
0   10   20   30   40   50

of Wexford, which has therefore become important. The streets are narrow and the houses small, and among them may still be seen that in which Cromwell lived after he had taken the town.

For Wexford, like Drogheda, was soon taken, and as at Drogheda, the defenders were slaughtered cruelly.

The weather had been wet and dreary, and Cromwell's camp was turned into a quagmire. Many of his soldiers fell ill. But as soon as Wexford was taken, he was on the march again to New Ross. Along the muddy roads, and by the bare fields of barley stubble they went to the little agricultural town on the river Barrow.

Cromwell began at once to bombard the town. But the news of the massacre of Drogheda and of Wexford had reached the garrison. The fear of Cromwell was upon them, and in three days they yielded. This time the soldiers were allowed to march out, leaving their arms and ammunition behind them. Some of the garrison were English, and five hundred of them immediately joined Cromwell. He was very glad to have them, for many of his own men had died, worn out by the long marches and terrible wet weather.

Chapter 24

MORE CONQUESTS IN IRELAND

CORK, Kinsale, and other towns, following the example of New Ross, yielded to Cromwell's generals. Cork is the third city in Ireland, and the most important in the south. The county of Cork, which is the largest in Ireland, is rich and fertile. In the west are mountains, and, sloping to the sea, beautiful valleys. Cork itself is a busy place. Besides being the largest butter market in the United Kingdom, it is the port by which the agricultural and dairy produce of the county finds its way to other lands. It has also breweries and distilleries, woollen, linen, paper, copper and tin factories.

Kinsale has a good harbour. It is a quaint old town with steep and winding streets, not changed very much perhaps since the days of Cromwell. It is a military and naval station, and every year the Royal Naval Reserve hold manœuvres here.

The Old Head of Kinsale is a point which runs out into the sea south-west of Kinsale. It is interesting as the first glimpse of "home" seen by travellers returning from America.

Soon after taking Wexford, Cromwell turned to Waterford, one of the oldest towns in Ireland. It is a seaport, and does great trade in live cattle and agricultural produce with Bristol, being the outlet for the fertile valleys of the county.

And now before the walls of Waterford, Oliver's triumphant course was stopped. The walls were strong, the defenders brave, and they would not give in. Winter was fast coming on. The country round was wasted and deserted. The rain poured in torrents. Food grew scarce. Cold, wet, and hungry, many of Cromwell's men became ill, many died. The Lord-General himself fell ill. Still he hoped when his heavy guns arrived to take the town. But the guns stuck fast in roads knee-deep in mud, and could not be brought to bear upon the town.

So at last Cromwell was forced to leave Waterford untaken, and march his sick and weary soldiers away to more comfortable winter quarters. On the 2nd of December they went, "it being so terrible a day as ever I marched in all my life," says Cromwell. Thus, worn and fever-stricken, the Ironsides scattered to Cork, Kinsale, Youghal, Wexford, Bandonbridge and other towns, for rest and shelter.

But in less than two months, Cromwell and his men, rested and refreshed, were again in the field. This time they marched inland. Town after town, castle after castle, yielded to the terror of Oliver's dreadful name, or if they would not yield, were taken with fearful slaughter.

Cashel, a little town which lies huddled at the foot of a rock rising sheer out of the fertile plain around, was taken. It was once the city of the kings of Munster. The stone upon which they sat to be crowned may still be seen, with other ancient relics upon the top of the rock.

Caher, on the Suir, one of the strongest fortresses in all Ireland, fell too. Fethard, where still many of the walls and gateways may be seen as they then were, was taken, and many another town of the rich wheat-lands of Tipperary.

In Kilkenny county, too, many a town fell. But at Kilkenny itself, the largest inland town in Ireland, Cromwell met with stout resistance. Kilkenny has grown to be a large town because it lies near one of the few coal fields in Ireland. It has also quarries of black marble, and is full of interest because of its old buildings, among which is a round tower.

There are many of these round towers in Ireland. For a long time people did not know for what they had been used. Now most people think that they were meant for bell towers to the monasteries and the churches. They were also used as watch-towers, and, in times of danger, as fortresses. There are still about seventy of them left in Ireland, some of them at least as old as the ninth century.

When Oliver arrived before Kilkenny he ordered the town to surrender as usual. "I am commanded to maintain this city for His Majesty, which, by the power of God, I am resolved to do," replied the governor. He would not give in, and the fight began. But a terrible sickness was raging within the walls, cutting down far more of the brave defenders than Cromwell's bullets. So at length the garrison was forced to yield. Cromwell allowed them to march out with colours flying and all the honours of war. It was only an empty honour, however, as two miles beyond the town they were obliged to lay down their arms.

Chapter 25

OLIVER'S LAST DAYS IN IRELAND

CLONMEL was the place which held out longest and which Cromwell found hardest to take. It is one of the busiest and cleanest (for many Irish towns are not famous for cleanliness) inland towns of Ireland. It is on the river Suir and on the borders of Tipperary and Waterford. As it lies in the middle of an agricultural district, it does great trade in grain and butter. Much grain is ground here, too, in the mills worked by the water of the Suir. The scenery here, as in many places in Ireland, is very beautiful, and visitors come long distances to see it.

Now, under the shadow of the hills Cromwell's Ironsides lay. Up and down the valleys roared and echoed his cannon. Day after day the walls trembled and shook beneath the awful thunder of shot and shell, until at last a breach was made. Then the Ironsides rushed to the walls, hoping to storm the town. But the defenders met them with such a hail of fire that they fell back again. Again and again they rushed to the attack. Again and again they fell back with sadly thinned ranks before that blazing fire of shot. Night fell, and still the town was untaken, and many an Ironside lay dead around the battlements.

But the brave defenders could hold out no longer. So hot and sharp had been their fire that their powder and shot were all done. In the dead of night they crept away, and next day the mayor of the town yielded it to Cromwell. He was angry when he found that the garrison had escaped. But he did not put the rest of the people to death. Thus Clonmel, too, came into Oliver's hands. But it had cost more men to take than any other town in all Ireland.

While Cromwell had been fighting and conquering in the south, another Parliamentarian army had been fighting and conquering in the north. Belfast, the most important town in all Ireland, had been taken. Although Belfast is not the real capital of Ireland, it is the trade capital, and also the capital of the province of Ulster. It stands upon a field of iron ore, and lying as it does opposite the Ayrshire coast, it can import coal easily from Scotland. The harbour is one of the best in the kingdom, and although there are some sand-banks in the lough, there is good anchorage, sheltered both on north and west by hills.

The graving docks of Belfast are the largest in the world. A graving dock is a dock into which a ship is put when the hull requires mending. When the ship has been sailed into the dock, the gates are shut and then the water is pumped out. The sides of the dock are like steps, and, as the water is drawn off, wooden props are placed against these steps and the sides of the ship, to prevent it heeling over. "Graves" is what is left at the bottom of the pan in melting tallow. "To grave "a ship means to smear the hull with this, but pitch is now used instead of graves.

There are also shipbuilding yards at Belfast, where some of the largest steamers afloat have been built. It has all kinds of imports and exports also, and the factories are almost too many to remember. There are iron foundries, distilleries, breweries, cable and rope factories, bacon-curing, and biscuit-making, and many other things. But the chief industry is linen-weaving. All over Ulster flax is grown, and Belfast is the centre of the linen trade. Linen has been woven in Ireland for at least seven hundred years, and Irish linens and Irish lace are famous all the world over.

Londonderry, too, is a good port, and famous for its linen. But here the chief trade is in shirts. As many as twenty thousand people, mostly women, work at making them. Londonderry had already been in the hands of the Parliamentarians when Cromwell landed, and now that Belfast and the country round was taken, all the east of Ireland, from Lough Foyle in the north to Cape Clear in the south, except Waterford, was held for Parliament.

All the west was still unconquered, but the west is the poorest part of Ireland. Then, there were no large towns there. The people lived in huts built of rough stones and turf, and were very wild and ignorant. It was a land of bog and mountain. The ports on the west look away from the Continent, and, although they look towards America and the New World, the roads and railways inland are not good. So that even were goods landed there, they are not easily carried away to other places. Nor is it easy to bring them from far inland to the shore.

This is not true, however, of Limerick. It lies near the mouth of the Shannon, which flows, connected by a long chain of navigable lakes, right through the heart of Ireland. It does an immense trade in bacon, and, as every one knows, is famous for its beautiful lace. Limerick was still untaken, but Cromwell decided to go home and leave it, and Waterford, and the west to be taken by his son-in-law Ireton. Oliver had been nine months in Ireland, and for many weeks letters had been coming, praying him to return to England, for he was needed there. So now he went, leaving behind him a name to be hated and cursed by Irishmen for many a year to come.

Chapter 26

OLIVER'S SECOND VISIT TO SCOTLAND

WHEN Cromwell returned to England he landed at Bristol, which is the port through which nearly all the Irish trade with England passes. In the old days, Bristol was very famous. It was from there that Cabot, and many another brave sailor, set out to discover and claim new lands in the west. From Bristol inland, roads easily pass from the Severn to the Thames valley, and so on to London. Thus, naturally, in early days, all the new trade of America passed through Bristol. But now Liverpool has beaten it, and most of the American trade goes to the Mersey.

When Cromwell arrived in London, everybody thronged to see him. The streets were packed with eager people, cheering wildly. Guns were fired and bells were rung.

"What a crowd has come to see your lordship's triumph," said some one.

"Yes, but if it were to see me hanged, how many more there would be," replied Oliver grimly.

There was little rest for the great soldier, for the Scots were again in arms.

The very day after the news of the death of King Charles had reached Edinburgh, they had proclaimed his son King. They would have nothing more to do with the English Parliament and the Union.

But the English Parliament resolved to have to do with them. And soon after Cromwell returned from Ireland, they commanded him and Fairfax to march into Scotland to fight the Scots. But Fairfax did not think it right to fight the Scots,

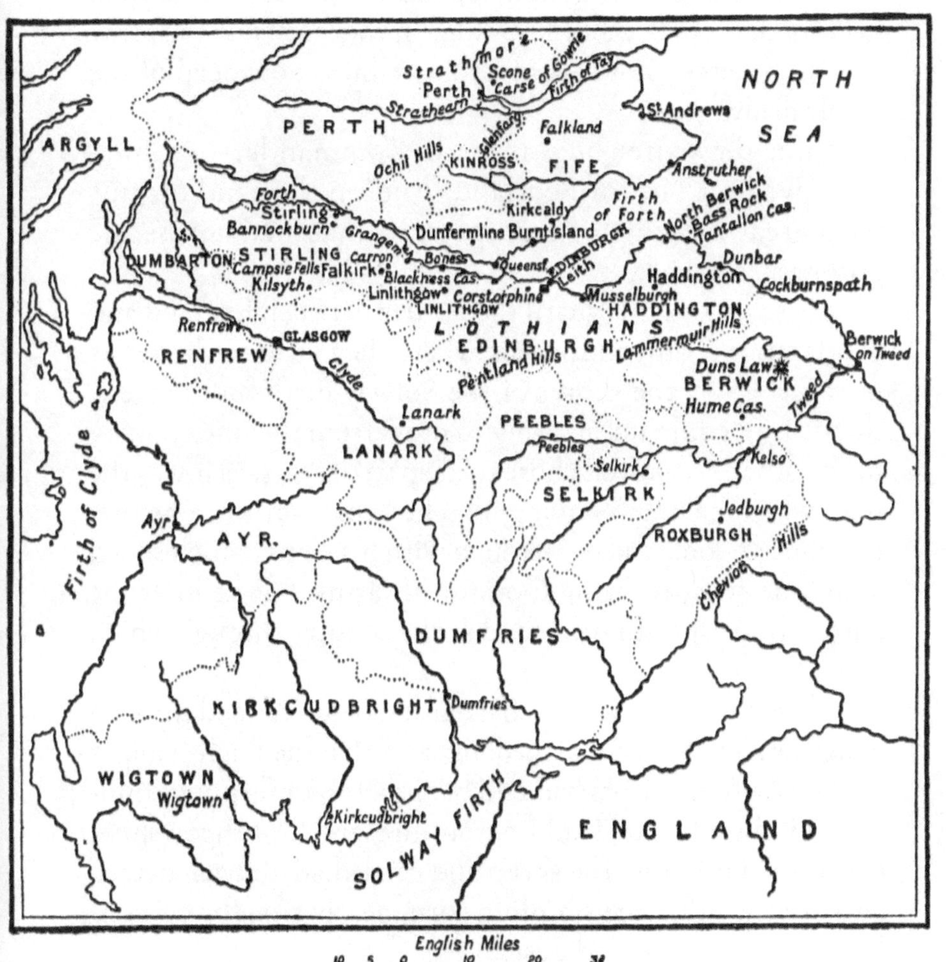

NORTH SEA
ARGYLL
PERTH
Strathmore
Scone
Carse of Gowrie
Perth
Firth of Tay
Stratheam
St. Andrews
Glenfarg
Falkland
Ochil Hills
KINROSS
FIFE
Anstruther
North Berwick
Forth
Firth
Bass Rock
Stirling
Kirkcaldy
of Forth
Tantallon Cas.
Bannockburn
Grangem.
Dunfermline Burntisland
Dunbar
STIRLING
Carron
Boness
EDINBURGH
Haddington
Cockburnspath
DUMBARTON
Campsie Fells
Falkirk
Blackness Cas.
Queensf.
Leith
Kilsyth
Linlithgow
Corstorphine
Musselburgh
HADDINGTON
LINLITHGOW
LOTHIANS
Renfrew
EDINBURGH
Lammermuir Hills
Berwick
GLASGOW
on Tweed
RENFREW
Clyde
Pentland Hills
Duns Law
BERWICK
Lanark
Hume Cas.
Tweed
PEEBLES
LANARK
Peebles
Selkirk
Kelso
Firth of Clyde
SELKIRK
Jedburgh
Ayr
ROXBURGH
AYR.
Cheviot Hills
DUMFRIES
KIRKCUDBRIGHT
Dumfries
ENGLAND
WIGTOWN
Wigtown
Kirkcudbright
SOLWAY FIRTH
English Miles
10 5 0   10   20   30

who had been friends so lately. So he laid down his command, and Oliver was made Captain-General and Commander-in-Chief of the whole Parliamentarian army. So at last he was both in name and in fact the greatest man in the kingdom. For ever since the King had been taken prisoner. and then beheaded, there had been no ruler in the land. But the army was the greatest power, and Cromwell was now head of the whole army.

Three days after he was made Commander-in-Chief, Cromwell set out for Scotland. And on the 22nd of July, with great blowing of trumpets, he marched across the border at Berwick.

The Cheviot Hills guard the border between England and Scotland. It is only in the east where they drop to the sea at Berwick, or by the shores of the Solway Firth on the west, that it is possible for an army to cross from the one country to the other. Cromwell chose to keep to the east, as it was the road which he knew, having marched that way once before. He wanted, too, to keep in touch with his ships, which sailed along the coast to bring food for his army. For he knew he dared not trust to finding food in the country through which he had to pass.

Oliver was right. It was a barren and deserted land through which he and his men marched. In order that the English might find no food, the Scots had laid bare their best farming counties, Edinburghshire, Haddingtonshire, and Linlithgowshire, called the Lothians. The sheep and cattle had all been driven away to the hills. The standing corn, nearly ripe for harvest, had been trampled and destroyed.

Keeping by the sea, the Ironsides marched on by a wild and beautiful valley to Cockburnspath, at the foot of the Lammermuir Hills. Then on again through the fruitful fields of Haddington. There a few weeks before the fields had been beautiful in the sunshine with the promise of a glorious harvest. Now the country was a barren desert.

Dunbar, with its now ruined castle standing on a rugged rock thrust out into the sea, was their next resting-place. Here the little port grew noisy and busy, while the ships unloaded the food brought for the army.

The next day, being thus provided, the Ironsides marched westwards, and inland to the town of Haddington, which, being in the midst of the best farming country of Scotland, is one of the centres of the grain trade. Next day, Sunday though it was, the Ironsides marched on again, for they had heard that the enemy was near. But they reached Musselburgh, near Edinburgh, with nothing more than a skirmish.

And here, between Leith and the Calton Hill, Cromwell found the Scots encamped. Their leader was General David Leslie, that same Leslie who at Marston Moor had fought side by side with Oliver, and helped him to turn defeat into victory. Now these two brave generals were arrayed against each other.

Leslie had gathered a good army. They numbered nearly half as many again as Cromwell's. But most of them were raw recruits, men brought from the plough and the harvest field, boys unused to war. For Scotland had not yet recovered the terrible blow dealt by Cromwell at Preston. Cromwell's army was full of tried men, the most perfect soldiers the world had ever seen.

Chapter 27.

THE BATTLE OF DUNBAR

LESLIE had taken up his position between the Calton and Leith, in order to guard Edinburgh, to keep Cromwell out of the port of Leith, and out of touch with his own supply ships as much as possible. It was a strong position, and for weeks Oliver tried to draw the Scottish general out of it. But wary Leslie would not come. There were skirmishes, assaults, and sallies, but no real battle.

Meanwhile both generals wrote letters to each other full of Bible texts. Both were sure that God was on their side, and would fight for them. From both camps rose the sounds of prayer and preaching, and the singing of psalms might be heard amidst the roar of cannon. Never were there stranger camps opposed to each other. It was as if two churches had come out to battle.

The weather became horribly wet. As the weeks passed the Ironsides suffered dreadfully. Sickness and famine thinned their ranks. Round and round Edinburgh prowled Oliver. Now he moved to the Pentland Hills, now to the village of Corstorphine, then again back to Musselburgh. At last, seeing the uselessness of it, he marched away again to Dunbar. His men were hungry, ragged, weary, and disheartened as they started upon their homeward march. It was a moonlight night, the 31st of August, and they did not go without some fighting, for the Scots fell upon them. "But the Lord by His providence put a cloud over the moon," and so the Ironsides reached the shelter of Dunbar in safety.

But next morning, on the hills around them, lay Leslie and his army, blocking the way south-ward. So here, on a little rocky point, between the sea and a deadly foe, lay Oliver and his men. "We are upon an engagement very difficult," he writes. "The enemy hath blocked up our way at the pass at Cockburnspath, through which we cannot get without almost a miracle. He lieth so upon the hills, that we know not how to come that way without great difficulty; and our lying here daily consumeth our men, who fall sick beyond imagination."

The case seemed almost desperate. Yet Oliver did not despair. "Indeed, we have much hope in the Lord," he says.

Then Leslie made his grand mistake.

Instead of waiting and watching, as he had done at Edinburgh, he began to move down hill. When Oliver saw what the enemy was about, he cried out, it is said, "Now hath the Lord delivered them into our hands." Then he made ready to fight.

All that night the armies lay opposite each other under the cloudy sky, where the harvest moon shone fitfully. The sea roared, and the shrill wind shrieked and whistled about them, and sudden dashes of rain soaked them, as they lay upon the bare ground, and now and again might be heard a soldier praying in the night.

At last morning came, and by four o'clock Oliver and his men were astir. Like ghosts they moved about quickly and silently in the dim shadowy light, getting into battle array. Soon they stood ready. "The Lord of Hosts!" was their battle cry, and so shouting, they rushed upon the foe.

At first the fight was fierce and stern. The silence of early dawn was broken by the roar of cannon, the crack and rattle of guns, and the clash of steel on steel. And over the tumult of war rose the strange battle cries, "The Covenant!" and "The Lord of Hosts!" Soon in the grey of dawn, the field lay red. Gallantly the Scotsmen fought, but they were for the most part untrained men. They could not stand against the Ironsides. Before an hour had passed their lines were broken.

"They run. I profess they run," cried Oliver.

At that moment the sun flung its first red beams across the grey and misty sea, and turning to it, in the joy of victory, Oliver cried, "Now, let God arise, and His enemies shall be scattered."

And so, shattered and broken, the Scots army fled in utter rout and confusion. The day was lost ere ever the sun was up.

Out of the depths Oliver had risen to a height of exultation. Calling a halt, he rallied his men, and bade them sing the 117th Psalm. For a moment the noise and clamour of battle was stilled, and through the quiet morning air came the sound of men's voices, hushing the groans of the dying, and rising upward a fit requiem for the dead.

> "O all ye nations of the world
> Praise ye the Lord always;
> And all the people everywhere
> Set forth His noble praise.
> "For great His kindness is to us,
> His truth doth ever live;
> Then to the Lord give praises great,
> Praise to Him ever give."

Then once more, the louder and more hideous for the pause, the roar of battle and chase broke forth.

It was a fearful rout. A thousand lay dead upon the field. Ten thousand more were taken prisoner. Much spoil, too, fell into the hands of the victors—colours, arms, guns, both great and small, indeed the whole baggage and train of the army.

Chapter 28

OLIVER GOES TO STIRLING AND TO GLASGOW

AFTER the battle of Dunbar, Cromwell returned to Edinburgh. There he lodged as an enemy in Moray House, where, a few years before, he had been received as an honoured guest. The castle of Edinburgh was held by the Royalist Scots, but at this time Oliver did not try to take it, and in a few days he marched northward, meaning to besiege Stirling.

Cromwell marched through Linlithgowshire, one of the finest farming counties in Scotland. He rode down the long street of the town of Linlithgow, which, like Northampton, is famous for its boots. It is famous, too, for its grand old palace, once the dwelling-place of kings. Now the town is quiet and sleepy, and the trade has drifted away to the towns and villages lying on the coal fields round, and to the rising port of Bo'ness. In the time of Cromwell Bo'ness was the second seaport in the kingdom, but afterwards it lost its trade and importance.

From Linlithgow Cromwell went to Falkirk, famous for its cattle-market or "tryst."

Falkirk now is a busy place. It lies on a coal field, and is near splendid farming country called the Carse. It is at the head of a canal joining the Forth and Clyde, and so does great trade with Glasgow. The famous Carron iron works are near, and the trade in coal and iron has made the port of Grangemouth grow rapidly.

From Falkirk Cromwell marched by the field of Bannockburn to within gunshot of Stirling.

In old times Stirling was a place of great importance.

It was the key of all the north, for it lies at the head of the Forth, where it becomes navigable. Its castle, built on a high rock rising sheer out of a fertile plain, held the pass between the Ochils on the north, and the Campsie Fells on the south.

Here kings have ruled, Parliaments have sat, and battles have been fought. Now the old glory of Stirling has passed away. It is no longer a dwelling-place of kings, but has become a manufacturing town, having both iron works and woollen manufactures.

But at this time, although Stirling was garrisoned, had Cromwell only known it, by "none but green new-levied so-jours," he did not take it but turned back again to Edinburgh.

At Linlithgow he made a halt. There he fortified the town and left a garrison, for he saw that from this town he could command Bo'ness and Blackness Castle, a strong fortress, farther down the coast.

Having stayed about three weeks in Edinburgh, Cromwell then marched across the country to Glasgow.

Glasgow is the trade capital of Scotland, and is the second city in the United Kingdom. In the hurry and bustle of its streets, in the noise and clamour of its river banks, in its smoke and fog and dirt, it is more like London than any other city. Glasgow has a splendid harbour with miles of quay and dock, where the largest ships afloat can lie. Yet there are men still living who can remember when it was possible to walk across the Clyde, where now these great vessels float. The bed of the river used to be wide and shallow, but rocks have been blown up and drilled out, tons of mud and stones have been scraped away, until the channel is now twenty-two feet deep. And still the work goes on, and every year masses of stone and mud are dredged from the river bed.

All this of course cost a great deal of money. But it had to be done if the trade of the west of Scotland was to succeed.

For the Firth of Clyde is the only great river estuary on the west, in the Lowlands. And here, in the Lowlands, lies the wealth of Scotland. Here are fertile plains, pastoral hills, and, above all, rich coal and iron fields. Upon these have grown up all kinds of factories, until the country, round Glasgow especially, has become one vast workshop, where the sky is dark with smoke-clouds and the air filled with the roar and clatter of machinery. And if all this industry was to prosper, an outlet for finished goods and an inlet for raw material had to be found near at hand.

Thus in Glasgow and the country round are crowded all the industries which in England are spread over many towns. The iron shipbuilding yards of the Clyde are more important now than those of the Thames or the Tyne. In Glasgow there are iron furnaces as great as those of South Wales. It has cotton factories like Manchester, woollen factories like Yorkshire, potteries, silk works, chemical works, metal works, and many other factories and industries. It is the natural centre of all the commerce and trade of the country round. It gives wealth and work to almost one-third of all the people of Scotland. Besides this it is a place of learning, having a University and a great Technical School.

But when Oliver and his soldiers came to Glasgow there was little of all this to be seen. It seemed to them "a very clean and well-formed town," and "though not so big nor so rich, yet to all seeming a much sweeter and more delightful place than Edinburgh, and would make a gallant head-quarters."

Chapter 29

THE STORY OF WILLIE WASTLE

OLIVER stayed only a "week-end" in Glasgow. On Sunday he went to church in the great cathedral, and listened to the preacher who railed against him and his soldiers, in a sermon two hours long. We can imagine the grim, stern soldier, with iron-grey hair, and face bronzed and deeply lined, sitting calm and unmoved, while the equally stern and fearless preacher called him "blasphemer "and "backslider."

But all who listened to him were not so patient. "Shall I pull him down? "asked one of Oliver's friends.

"No," replied he. "He is a fool and you are another. I will presently pay him in his own fashion."

And so he did, for he asked the preacher to dinner, and ended with a prayer lasting three hours.

Oliver's treatment of the Scots was very different from his treatment of the Irish. Here there was no butchery, as at Drogheda and Wexford. The Scots were godly men though mistaken, said Cromwell. He did not wish to conquer them but to bring peace between the two countries. Peace, it seemed, could only be brought by the sword; yet his "heart yearned after the godly in Scotland." "In Glasgow," says one writer, "Cromwell's soldiers behaved as if they had been in London."

When they returned to Edinburgh they did not go by the way they had come, by Kilsyth and Linlithgow, but through the uplands of Lanarkshire, by heathery moor and deep-wooded glens, now heavy with rain, then over the Pentlands to Edinburgh. "The worst march we have ever yet had homeward, over mountains and bogs such as no army ever passed," says one of them.

The winter was now near, the weather was very wet, so Oliver and his men took up winter quarters in Edinburgh. All this time Cromwell had been mining away at the rock of Edinburgh Castle, hoping to blow it up, if it would not yield. But he found it very hard, and the mines were of no use. Now he got some big guns and began to bombard the castle. But even that did little harm to the massive walls, and had the castle been held by a resolute man, Cromwell would perhaps never have been able to take it, for there was food enough to last many months within the walls.

But the governor was young and of no great courage. So on Christmas day he gave up the castle to Cromwell, marching out indeed with colours flying, but to be looked upon by his brother Scots as a traitor and a coward.

"Indeed the mercy is very great and seasonable," writes Cromwell. "I think I need say little of the strength of the place; which, if it had not come in as it did, would have cost very much blood to have attained, if at all to be attained."

During the winter there was much marching out, and marching back again, skirmishing, and taking of castles. Hume Castle, not far from Kelso, in Berwickshire, was one of the strongest of these. Berwickshire, like the Lothians, is a fertile county. In the north, on the slopes of the Lammermuirs, are sheep farms, and in the south, in the Merse plain of Tweed, there is good agricultural land. All about are dotted pleasant little villages, but there is not a large town in the whole county.

When Oliver sent a message to the governor of Hume Castle, ordering him to yield, he replied, "I know not Cromwell, and as for my castle, it is built upon a rock."

So the thunder of Cromwell's great guns began. Four days passed and still the governor would not yield. Instead he sent a scornful letter to Cromwell.

"I William of the Wastle,
Am now in my castle;
And aw the dogs in the town,
Shanna gar me gang down."

Still the bombardment went on, and at last a breach was made in the walls, strong though they were.

Then it was resolved to storm the castle, and Oliver's officers cast lots as to who should lead the attack. But now, seeing that it was useless to hold out any longer, the governor gave way. So Hume Castle was taken, and all its furniture and treasure was divided among the soldiers as spoil. Only the governor's wife was allowed to take away her bed and a few things belonging to herself.

But perhaps the most important castles taken were Tantallon, not far from North Berwick in Haddingtonshire, and Blackness on the shores of Forth. Blackness is one of the fortresses which by the articles of the Union we are obliged to keep garrisoned. It is now used as a powder magazine. North Berwick lies upon the Firth of Forth, just where it opens into the North Sea. Besides being a fishing-place with a good fishing harbour, it has fine sands, and a famous golf course, so many people go there every summer. The ruins of Tantallon Castle are still to be seen. The walls were so strong that "ding down Tantallon, and build a brig to the Bass," used to be a proverb, meaning that both were impossible.

But Tantallon is a ruin, and although there is no bridge to the Bass, quite as wonderful things as that have been done.

When these castles were taken nearly all the south of Scotland, from the Tweed to the Forth, was in the power of Cromwell. Only Stirling and the north held out.

Chapter 30

OLIVER VISITS A ROYALIST HOUSE

MEANTIME Cromwell became very ill. So ill indeed was he, that a little later he wrote, "I thought I should have died of this sickness; but the Lord seemeth to dispose otherwise."

He did not die. But only very slowly did he get better. At last he was out again, marching back and forth, as of old. One day, on his way from Glasgow, he stopped at the house of Sir Walter Stewart. Sir Walter was a Royalist, and was not at home. Perhaps he was away fighting for the King. But his wife and his little boy were there. The lady was a Royalist and did not love the "rebels," but she treated her visitor politely and gave him food and drink.

The great soldier was gentle and kindly to this Royalist lady. He talked to her in a friendly way, telling her that he too was a Stewart, for that had been his mother's name. He seemed so kind that the little boy, who was not very strong, and who had been shy of the soldiers, now came quite near and began to play with Oliver's sword handle. Then, perhaps thinking of his own grand-children whom he loved, Oliver laid his big brown hand upon the boy's head, stroking his curls gently. "You are my little captain," he said.

Then, after a little more friendly talk, and having said a long grace in thanks for his refreshment, Oliver went on his fighting way. But the lady, Royalist though she was, kept a kindly remembrance of the great rough soldier who had such gentle ways, and was never again so bitter as she had been against the "rebels."

Again and again Oliver fell ill. For the last nine years he

CROMWELL AND SIR WALTER STEWART.

had lived such a hard life in camp and field, fighting and working, that it was little wonder if at last his health broke down. Now Fairfax sent two doctors in his own coach from London, and the Parliament begged him to return home and rest a little. But Cromwell would not. He wanted to finish his work in Scotland. "My lord is not sensible that he has grown an old man," says one writer.

By July Oliver was much better, and he began in real earnest to try to draw the Scots out of their stronghold of Stirling. But wary Leslie was again in command. He had learned the lesson of Dunbar, and he sat still.

Then, as Cromwell could not draw Leslie out of Stirling, he made up his mind to go round behind him. He had plenty of vessels at command, so he shipped some of his army over the Forth, into Fifeshire. There was then of course no great railway bridge across the Forth at Queensferry, and trains were then unknown. The Forth Bridge, which was opened in 1890, is one of the engineering wonders of the world. Its spans are so high that ships can pass underneath, and the trade of ports lying farther up the river is uninjured.

The kingdom of Fife, as the county is sometimes called, is a peninsula formed by the Firth of Forth on the south, and the Firth of Tay on the north. It is one of the richest of Scottish counties, having both good soil for cultivation and coal fields, and, in consequence, manufactures.

The south, through which Cromwell's army now marched, is the busy manufacturing part. Here is Dunfermline, now noted for its table linen, but once, with its palace and abbey, famous as the dwelling and burial place of kings. Here too is Kirkcaldy with its linoleum factories, and many other towns.

Near Dunfermline there was a battle between the Parliamentarians and the Scots, in which the Scots were defeated. Cromwell was not there, but watched the battle from far off.

Then, having again marched in vain to Stirling, he decided to cross the Forth himself, leaving only a few troops to guard the country south of the Forth.

After he landed in Fifeshire, Cromwell besieged Burntisland. But the stout little place held out against him, and only yielded at last, it is said, on condition that he would pave the streets and repair the harbour.

The Parliamentarians now took complete possession of Fifeshire. One general marched along the coast seizing ships and guns. For all round the shores of Fife are busy towns and ports, where fishing is the chief industry, and of which Anstruther is the busiest.

Some of the troops marched to the north, where the fertile plain called the Howe of Fife stretches from St. Andrews to the Firth of Tay. There stands the ancient palace of Falkland, famous in the days when the Stewart kings used to go to hunt in the great forest of Falkland. While Cromwell's troops were there they set fire to part of the palace and cut down many of the fine old trees of the forest. Indeed so much of this forest was wasted during the Civil War that little of it remained. Thus having made Fife sure, Cromwell next marched through the beautiful Glen Farg to the walls of Perth.

Chapter 31

THE CROWNING MERCY

PERTHSHIRE lies in the very heart of Scotland. Only where the long arm of the Firth of Tay runs inland does it touch the sea. It is one of the largest and most beautiful of Scottish counties. The north-western part belongs to the Highlands, and there, is some of the grandest loch and mountain scenery in the whole country. Here rugged, heather-clad hills rise one behind another till they are lost in blue distance. Here deer roam upon the mountain sides, pheasants and grouse brood among the heather, and eagles nest in the craggy peaks. But of towns there are none, and of villages only a few, with, here and there, a lonely farm-house or shooting lodge. More than half of Perthshire indeed is deer forest and heath.

But in the valleys such as Strathmore and Strathearn are fertile fields. Here upon the gentle slopes strawberries and other fruits grow well, and corn and wheat ripen in the sunshine, while along the shores of the Tay stretches the Carse of Gowrie, famous as a farming district.

Perth itself is the only town of any size in the whole county. It is now chiefly famous for its dye works. But it used to be a town of great importance. The kings of Scotland often lived here, and at the Abbey of Scone, near, they were crowned. And here, but six months before Cromwell arrived at the gates of Perth, the Scots had crowned Charles II.

Beyond Stirling, Perth holds the chief passes of the north, and Cromwell knew that if he could take it, he would cut off Stirling from the supplies of food, which were brought to it from the north. When that was done Stirling would be forced to yield.

Oliver's task was easy. The men of Perth showed no fight. He had lain before the town only one day when they yielded to him. But scarcely had Cromwell entered the town, when the news arrived that Charles and his army had left Stirling, and were marching for England. Cromwell had needed nearly all his men to overrun Fife and take Perth, so that the way south had been left open for Charles, did he choose to take it.

As soon as Cromwell heard the news, he left a few thousand men under General Monk to guard Perth and take Stirling, and dashed after Charles.

Charles went by the west, crossing into England at one end of the Cheviots by the Solway Firth; Cromwell went by the east, as he had come.

For nearly a month they chased each other, as it were, Charles marching through the sheep-farming counties of Peebles and Dumfries, with their busy woollen manufacturing towns. He crossed into England near Carlisle, famous for its castle and cathedral, and so often the scene of Border fights. Day after day he marched on, among the beautiful hills and lakes of Cumberland and Westmorland. Then came a change of scene as he passed through busy, smoky Lancashire to the pasture lands of Cheshire Plain and Shropshire. He kept by the borders of Wales, for he hoped that there many Cavaliers would join his army. But he was disappointed, and striking south-west again he made for the Royalist town of Worcester.

Worcester was among the first towns to declare for Charles I. It was among the last to yield to the Parliament. And now it gladly opened its gates to Charles II.

Worcestershire is part of a valley lying between the mountains of Wales and the Northamptonshire Upland. For hundreds of years it has been famous for its hop and fruit gardens. Plums, pears, and apples are chiefly grown, and a great deal of cider is made.

Worcester itself is also famous for its china factory, its potted lampreys, its sauce, and many other things.

The Royalists of England had not risen to join Charles as he had hoped, and his army now hardly numbered sixteen thousand. So here in this city of the fruitful plain he rested his weary men. And here Oliver with about thirty thousand men closed round him.

It was the 28th of August when Cromwell appeared before Worcester, but not until the 3rd of September—his lucky day—was the great battle fought, which was to be the ruin of the Royalist cause.

In the early morning of the 3rd, Cromwell, with the skill of a great commander, began to post his men. But not until the afternoon did the grand struggle come. Then for hours the battle raged, first without the wall of Worcester, then within. Oliver himself rode with his men; "My lord-general did exceedingly hazard himself, riding up and down in the midst of the fire," says one who saw.

It was a fierce contest, but when at last, far into the night, the noise of battle died away, the cause of Charles was utterly lost, the Scots army utterly shattered. Three thousand lay dead upon the field. Ten thousand more were prisoners, among them nearly half the nobles of Scotland.

That night, Charles fled away a homeless wanderer and after many dangers he escaped to France. That night, Cromwell, his great enemy, sheathed his sword, never to draw it again. He had fought his last battle and won his last victory, his "Crowning Mercy" he called it. For nine years Oliver had been a soldier. In those nine years he had created an army, and with it had conquered three kingdoms and a principality. In those nine years he had risen from being a simple unknown farmer to be the chief man in the land. In those nine years he had made for himself a name which will never be forgotten as long as history is read.

Chapter 32.

TAKE AWAY THAT BAUBLE

WHEN Oliver returned from Worcester, the Speaker and the whole Parliament, the Lord Mayor and aldermen of London, and a great throng of people came out to meet him. With much rejoicing and shouting, with firing of guns and beating of drums, the conqueror was led through the streets. Hampton Court was given to him to live in, and £4000 a year of public money was voted to him.

The war was now at last truly over. But all the country was in confusion. The prisons were full. Hundreds of law cases were waiting to be tried, but there was no justice anywhere. The land was one wide desert of misery and beggary.

Yet Parliament did little or nothing. Members made long-winded and learned speeches, but without a true leader they seemed unable to act. In this way a year and a half passed. Once more the army grew impatient of the Parliament. They declared that this Parliament had sat long enough, and that it was worn out and useless. They said it no longer spoke the mind of the people, and that the members must now resign, and allow a new Parliament to be chosen. "I told them," said Cromwell later, "that the nation loathed their sitting."

But the members had no wish to resign. They brought in a bill, indeed, by which some new members were to be elected, but the old members were to keep their seats. This made the army more angry still, and they resolved that this bill should not pass.

One day, as Cromwell and his officers were sitting in council, a breathless messenger arrived to tell them that even now the Parliament was passing the hated bill.

At first Cromwell would not believe the news. But a second and then a third messenger came. Then Oliver rose. "It is not honest. Yea, it is against common honesty," he cried out, and then he left the room. He told no one where he was going or what he meant to do.

He was no longer dressed like a soldier, in scarlet or buff coat and breastplate of steel. He wore black clothes and a tall black hat and grey woollen stockings, like some quiet citizen. Thus plainly dressed he called a company of his men and marched to the House.

Leaving the soldiers without, he entered and took his seat, with his hat on.

For some time he sat quietly listening to the talk. Then, just as the bill was about to be passed, he rose in his place, and, taking off his hat, began to speak. At first he spoke calmly, then, growing more and more angry, he told the members that they were bad and useless, thinking only of themselves, and that they had become tyrants and the supporters of tyrants. "Yea," he cried, "the Lord hath done with you and hath chosen other instruments for the carrying on of his work who are more worthy."

Then another member rose. "This is strange language," said he, "strange language, and utterly unbecoming in a trusted servant."

But Oliver had now risen to a white passion of wrath. Crushing his hat upon his head, he strode out into the floor of the House. "You are no Parliament," he cried, stamping his foot. "I say you are no Parliament. Come, come, I will put an end to your prating. Call them in! Call them in!" and again he stamped.

The door opened, and twenty or thirty grim soldiers marched in.

"This is not honest," cried one of the members, using the

very words which Oliver himself had used a short time before. "Yea, it is against morality and common honesty." But Cromwell in a fury of passion replied with scoffing words.

"Begone," he cried, "you have sat here too long. It is time to give way to honester men." Then, as one by one, the members passed out, he flung all manner of taunts at them, calling some "drunkards," others "unjust persons, evil livers."

The House was nearly empty, but the Speaker would not go. That same Speaker who had defied Charles now defied Oliver.

"Fetch him down," cried he.

"Come, sir, I will lend you a hand," said one of Cromwell's friends.

So the Speaker left the chair.

Then catching sight of the mace as it lay upon the table, "What shall we do with this bauble?" cried Oliver. "Here, take it away."

So the mace was removed.

The House was now empty, and Oliver, seizing the hated bill, put it under his cloak. Then locking the door he marched away. Thus on 10th April 1653 was the Long Parliament ended. It had lasted twelve years.

Chapter 33

THE LORD PROTECTOR

LESS than three months after Cromwell had turned the Parliament out of doors he called another. This time he and his friends chose all the members, and they hoped that things would now be done as they wished. But soon it was seen that this new Parliament was not much better than the last. In six months the Little Parliament, as it was called, was dismissed. It is sometimes called Praise-God Barebones Parliament, from the name of one of the members.

It was now almost five years since King Charles had been beheaded. Yet the country had chosen no ruler. Oliver indeed by the strength of his own character and will had become the foremost man. He was Commander-in-Chief of the Army and Lord-Lieutenant of Ireland, but he was not, in name, governor of Great Britain.

Now it was resolved that he should really be acknowledged as ruler.

Dressed in black velvet, and wearing a gold band round his hat, Oliver received in state the Lord Mayor, judges, and magistrates of the city of London. With his hand on the Bible, he promised to keep the liberties of the people. Then with the sword of office carried before him, and all around him bareheaded, he only wearing his hat, he was led to Whitehall, which was henceforth to be his house of state.

Oliver was now King in all but name. Indeed had he so chosen he might have been crowned as King. But he knew that the army hated the name of King, so he chose instead the title of Lord Protector. He kept great state and signed himself Oliver P., just as King he would have written Oliver R.

CROMWELL AS LORD PROTECTOR.

The triumph of Oliver's life had come. But to him it brought no rest. He had laid down the sword only to take up the sceptre. The next five years were years of ceaseless toil. He fought his Parliaments as he had fought his enemies in the field. Not for the last time were the doors of the House locked. Not for the last time had the tramp of armed men sounded in the lobby and upon the staircase. Oliver was a tyrant such as no Tudor or Stewart had ever been. Yet he was a man of so great mind that he used his power, not for his own pleasure, but for the good of the people.

He brought order out of hopeless confusion. The country settled to rest and quiet. Trade and commerce returned. Evil was punished, justice was done, and not only that, learning was encouraged and a life of quiet culture became once more possible in England.

In Scotland, one writes, "we always reckon those eight years of the usurpation a time of great peace and prosperity." In Ireland, alas, it was different, and the bitterness of Cromwell's rule there has never been forgotten.

But great though Oliver was at home he was greater still abroad. Never since the days of Elizabeth had England stood so high. Her ships were victorious on every sea. The Protestant nations of all the world looked to Oliver as their protector, and kings and princes were glad of his friendship and in fear of his anger.

Yet in the midst of all his grandeur Oliver was humble. Once he said, "I can say in the presence of God, in comparison with whom we are but poor creeping ants upon the earth, that I would have been glad to have lived under my woodside, to have kept a flock of sheep, rather than undertake such a government as this."

Oliver, like all strong men, had his enemies. There were many who hated him, and during the years of his rule there were constant plots to murder him. But the plots were always discovered.

Milton, one of our great poets, lived at the same time as Oliver, and was his friend. He wrote a poem about him at this time:—

> "Cromwell, our chief of men, who through the cloud
> Not of war only, but detractions rude,
> Guided by faith and matchless fortitude,
> To peace and truth thy glorious way hast ploughed,
> And on the neck of crowned fortune proud
> Hast reared God's trophies, and his work pursued,
> While Darwen's stream, with blood of Scots imbrued,
> And Dunbar field, resounds thy praises loud,
> And Worcester's laureate wreath: yet much remains
> To conquer still; Peace hath her victories
> No less renowned than War: new foes arise,
> Threatening to bind our souls with secular chains.
> Help us to save free conscience from the paw
> Of hireling wolves, whose gospel is their maw."

In the midst of his greatness and splendour Oliver had his own sorrows and troubles too. Many of his friends died, some forsook him, and now, in the summer of 1658, his best loved daughter Elizabeth died, after suffering great pain.

Her death struck like a blow at the heart of Oliver, for he had always been a loving father. All through his letters we find tender words and messages about his children. Sometimes it is "Dick "he speaks of, sometimes his little "wenches," his "little girls" and their "brats." In all his greatness he never lost his simple love of wife and children.

Now, broken with sorrow and bowed with many labours, the great Protector lay dying. The hearts of his friends were filled with sadness, and the churches were thronged with praying multitudes. But his hour had come.

One night a fearful storm burst over land and sea. A wild wind howled and shrieked around the stately palace where Oliver lay. It lashed the sea into white, cruel foam, shattering ships and strewing the shores with wreckage. It tore through forest and town, uprooting mighty trees, and unroofing houses, until at last its fury was spent.

And in the calm which followed, the great Protector sank to rest. "My work is done," he said.

He died upon the 3rd of September, the day of Dunbar and Worcester, his lucky day.

www.ingramcontent.com/pod-product-compliance
Lightning Source LLC
Chambersburg PA
CBHW031004210726
48290CB00007B/2464